In his time on the police force, Mitch had never felt more helpless with a case than this one.

The newspapers were calling for Fala to be caught, and the citizens of Oxford were frightened where he would strike next.

Mitch had to find the link to these murders. He mentally checked off the clues: bloody handprints, a knife, a truck, a blond hair and C.J. The last one hit him like a punch in the stomach. For some unknown reason Fala had chosen to put her in the middle of the worst murder spree in the history of Oxford.

Chills raced up Mitch's spine as he wondered what Fala had planned next for C.J. He had to find Fala. No way was he going to let C.J. end up as the next victim.

"If you want to get to her," Mitch muttered, "you'll have to kill me first."

SANDRA ROBBINS,

a native West Tennessean, was a teacher and principal in Tennessee public schools. She now writes full-time and is an adjunct college professor. She is married and has four children and five grandchildren.

Her fascination with mystery and suspense can be traced to all the Nancy Drew books she read as a child. She hopes her stories will entice readers to keep turning the page until wrongs have been righted and romance has blossomed in her characters' lives.

It is her prayer that God will use her words to plant seeds of hope in the lives of her readers. Her greatest desire is that many will come to know the peace she draws from her life verse, Isaiah 40:31—*But those who hope in the Lord will renew their strength. They will soar on wings like eagles, they will run and not grow weary, they will walk and not be faint.*

To find out more about Sandra and her books, go to her Web site at http://sandrarobbins.net.

FINAL WARNING

SANDRA ROBBINS

Steeple
Hill®

Published by Steeple Hill Books™

STEEPLE HILL BOOKS

Steeple
Hill®

Recycling programs
for this product may
not exist in your area.

ISBN-13: 978-0-373-44352-9

FINAL WARNING

www.SteepleHill.com

Printed in U.S.A.

If we believe not, yet he abideth faithful:
he cannot deny himself.
—*2 Timothy* 2:13

To the memory of DJ Stewart "Stewman" Byars, who gave hours of enjoyment to his listeners. Without his invaluable information this book wouldn't have been possible.

Acknowledgments

Special thanks to Paul Tinkle, President and General Manager of Thunderbolt Broadcasting, for opening the doors of WCMT and giving me a behind-the-scenes look at the world of radio.

To Chris Brinkley, thank you for answering my questions and allowing me to experience live broadcasting as a part of Good Times in the Morning with Chris and Paul.

ONE

Let's play a game, C.J.

Her skin prickled at the words in the subject line of the e-mail. C. J. Tanner's finger hovered over the delete key, but she pulled away, unable to press it. She clicked the mouse, and the message came into view.

Let's play a game, I'll send a clue,
The hidden answer must come from you.
To win a round you have to know
Where I will strike a deadly blow.
Fala

The strange message made no sense. A deadly blow?

As the talk show host of *C.J's Journal* on WLMT radio, she'd received lots of creepy messages. But this one was different. How, she didn't know, but it made every nerve ending in her body tingle.

The angry remarks from callers to her show flashed into her mind. Perhaps the e-mail was from Jimmy Carpenter. Maybe he didn't like his suspected illegal drug activities being discussed by listeners of her program. One caller the night before had been irate because the police had only been able to charge Jimmy with drug possession during his latest arrest. To make matters worse, the caller had said Jimmy made bail right away and was probably already peddling his drugs on the streets of Oxford, Tennessee.

The shrill ring of the telephone jolted her from her thoughts as it pierced the morning quiet. Her heart still pumping in fear, her hand snaked toward the phone, but struck the coffee cup sitting next to the computer. With a cry, she steadied the mug with both hands before picking up the handset.

"H-hello," she said.

"C.J., this is Mitch. How are you?"

She gripped the handset more tightly and closed her eyes as the soothing tone of her ex-fiancé's voice poured over her. She wanted to cry out her relief that he'd called, but she bit her lip. He'd been the first person she'd allowed a peek into her heart, and now she was suffering the consequences of that choice.

As she'd done so often during the last month, she raised her left hand and stared at it. No longer did the emerald-cut diamond ring sparkle on her finger. When Mitch Harmon proposed, they had promised to love each other forever. It only took six months to dash her hopes of finally finding the happily-ever-after she'd always wanted.

She took a deep breath. "I'm okay, Mitch. How about you?"

There was a moment of hesitation before he spoke. "I'm fine."

His image rippled through her mind. She wondered how he looked. Had he slept well, or were his eyes tired from lack of sleep, as hers were? "That's good. Is there any special reason for your call?"

He released a long breath. "I wanted to tell you that I've been listening to your radio show."

What a surprise. This was very different from his reaction when she first told him of the addition of *C.J.'s Journal* to the

WLMT schedule. It was the type of program she'd dreamed about—a talk show five days a week in the prized afternoon drive time of radio.

She frowned. "I'm glad. Especially after you've been so insistent on my not doing the show. What was it you said? That I'd attract all kinds of crazy callers."

"That's right, and I haven't changed my mind about that." She could imagine his clenched jaw and the thin line of his mouth. She'd seen that expression often enough during their disagreements over the radio program. "It's just that I see the dark side of life in Oxford every day. I don't want you to be put in any danger," he said.

C.J. closed her eyes and rubbed her fingers across her forehead. The memory of all the arguments of the past few months flashed into her mind. He'd been adamant that she shouldn't do the show, and she'd been just as determined to show him and everybody else that she was up to the task. "We've been over this before, Mitch. I know you don't want me to do this program, but I'm not giving it up."

"I'm worried about you, and I miss you. It's even starting to affect my work. I can't concentrate, and that's not good for a policeman."

C.J.'s skin prickled, and she sat up straighter in the chair. "Well, we wouldn't want to put Myra in any danger, would we?"

"What's that supposed to mean?" Surprise laced his words.

C.J. almost laughed at how slow on the uptake Mitch could be sometimes. Myra Summers, his partner, had been in love with him ever since they began working together. Everybody but Mitch knew it. C.J. hadn't worried about it then because she knew Mitch loved her, but now Myra waited to pick up the pieces. A knifelike pain sliced through C.J.'s heart at the thought.

"I'm sure your partner has offered you a nice shoulder to cry on."

Mitch gave a slight gasp. "Is that really why you broke our engagement? You're jealous of Myra? For your information, she's been a good friend."

C.J. started to offer a retort, but suddenly she felt tired. She didn't want to fight anymore. He would never understand how important her radio program was to her. "I need to go. I have to get ready for work."

"Fine." He was all business now. "But one more thing."

"What?"

"Be careful with your editorials on the show. There are some dangerous characters in this town. It wouldn't be wise to make them angry."

Like Fala, she thought. For a moment she wanted to tell Mitch about the e-mail, but she bit her lip. "I will be, Mitch. Goodbye."

She hung up the phone and sat at the desk, thinking about all the time she and Mitch had spent together. When they first met, he'd just been promoted to detective on the police force, and she was a struggling assistant to the producer at the radio station. She often wondered why he had chosen her.

With his dark hair, eyes like pools of rich chocolate, and shoulders as broad and strong as a college running back, he was too handsome for someone as plain as her.

He had often told her she was the most beautiful woman he'd ever known, but she knew better. For years her mother had expressed the truth on a regular basis. The words were branded into her mind as if they'd been spoken yesterday. *Get out of my sight, you repulsive little creature.* She had hoped her love for Mitch would erase those memories, but it hadn't.

They had been so much in love, or at least she thought he had loved her. Apparently, she'd been wrong about that. A man who loves a woman should support her decisions, not try to control her by imposing his own ideas of what was best for her.

No man would ever treat her the way her father treated her mother. C.J. had escaped his rages, which often sent her mother to the hospital, but she couldn't forget them. Those memories had never been far from her mind while she worked her way through college and landed her first job. She'd fought for everything she'd gotten in life, and she would never be manipulated and controlled by a man.

Not that Mitch would ever hit her. He was too kind for that. In fact, he talked to her about God's love all the time and how he wanted her to feel the peace that came from believing. She laughed and told him she'd prayed often when she was a little girl. At night she'd cower under the covers and beg God to make her father stop hitting her mother, but it never worked. She'd given up on God a long time ago.

With a sigh she reached to turn off the computer, but her gaze returned to the strange message on the screen. If Fala's intent had been to scare her, he'd accomplished this task.

Erase the message—that's what she had to do. Then she could forget about it. Her fingers punched the delete key, and the words disappeared.

No sense of relief came. Instead a strong wind shook the house and sent an icy chill flowing through her body. Her heart pounded at the mournful song the gusts whistled in the eaves—*deadly blow, deadly blow.*

Twenty minutes later, C.J. backed her car out of the garage and down the driveway. Adam Connor waved at her from the sidewalk in front of his house across the street. She pulled to the curb and rolled the window down. Adam jogged toward her, the morning newspaper under his arm. His brown eyes and dark, straight hair, combined with his year-round tan, reminded her of a young George Hamilton.

He peered inside, his white teeth flashing behind his broad

smile. "Morning, C.J. You must be running late. You're usually gone when I get back from the gym."

"I *am* late, but I wanted to welcome you home. When did you get back from Atlanta?"

Damp strands of his black hair clung to his forehead, and he wiped at them with his hand. "Last night. I sold my paintings and have some commissions for more."

"Wonderful. We'll have to get together and celebrate your success. I'll invite Gwen. She's really missed you."

A shy smile curled his lips at the mention of Gwen Anderson, C.J.'s assistant. "I've missed her, too. When you get to work, tell her I got in late last night, but I'll call her later."

"Will do."

He raised his eyebrows and leaned closer. "But what about you? Any news about you and Mitch?"

She tugged at her seat belt. "No, everything's still the same as when you left."

His smile turned to a frown. "I'm sorry, C.J."

She placed her hand on the gearshift. "Well, work calls. I'll talk to you later."

Adam waved and backed away. She glanced in the rearview mirror to return the wave but hesitated, a sense of unease filling her. An unfamiliar black SUV was parked across the street from her house. She could barely make out the person behind the wheel, but it appeared to be a woman.

Her fingers tightened around the steering wheel. Could Fala be a woman? Fear rose in her throat and she swallowed, then relaxed. She was being silly. If she started worrying about every message she received, it would affect her work. Besides, the e-mail was just somebody's idea of a joke. She pressed the accelerator and turned her attention to the morning traffic.

Juggling a cup of coffee in one hand and her briefcase in the other, C.J. stopped in front of the closed door to her office on the second floor of the WLMT radio station building. Gwen Anderson, her blond hair bouncing on her shoulders, hurried forward.

"Let me get that for you." She opened the door and motioned C.J. to enter. "What are assistants for if they can't assist the boss when she's loaded down?"

Pert. That was the only word C.J. had ever been able to come up with to describe Gwen, whose blue eyes always sparkled behind the oversize glasses she wore. She had boundless energy that never seemed to flag. And her intuition! Gwen could foresee an assignment and complete it even before it was given to her. Gwen was a jewel among the staff of WLMT.

C.J. entered the office and set her coffee on the edge of the desk. She dropped the briefcase next to her cup and sank into her chair. "Thanks for the help, but you know I don't think of myself as your boss. I've never had a better working relationship with anyone."

Gwen eased into a chair across from C.J. "I should thank you every day for giving me this chance. I sure wouldn't have gotten it if it'd been left up to our esteemed producer."

C.J. tilted her head and arched an eyebrow. "Harley appreciates your work."

A snort of disgust came from Gwen's throat. "Sure he does. That's why he's been so quick to recommend me for a raise."

"Now, Gwen. You know that's Mr. Cunningham's decision. Harley's just our producer."

C.J. leaned back in her chair. "I know you don't like him, but he's really been good to me. This new show is just what I needed."

Darkness the color of storm clouds flashed in Gwen's eyes. "Don't be taken in by him. He thinks he's the most important person around here. Can't get along with any department. He calls the engineering guys idiots, and they take it out on us. I can't get anything repaired—not even my printer."

This wasn't the first time C.J. had heard employees complaining about Harley. Every few days someone asked her to intervene in a conflict with him. Gwen was just the latest in a long line. "I'll talk to Matt in engineering."

Gwen crossed her arms and frowned. "While you're at it, ask him about the WLMT sign. Ever since I was a child I've loved driving by here at night and seeing those tall letters standing on the flat roof of the building. They used to light up the sky, but not anymore. Have you seen it lately?"

The sign had been the trademark of their station for years, but like a lot of things around the building, it had fallen into disrepair. "Yeah, I noticed the other night the *T* was the only letter lit."

Gwen nodded. "Right. You never know which letters will be illuminated. I came by here last night, and the sign was completely out. Now this morning it's fine. How do you explain that?"

"Harley said there's a short in it, but the company that's supposed to fix it keeps putting us off."

"Good morning, lovely ladies. Did I hear my name mentioned?" Harley Martin, his wire-rimmed glasses propped on his head, stuck his hands in the pockets of his wrinkled pants and stepped into the room. His potbelly hung over the waistband and his belt looped underneath the bulging girth. He stopped next to Gwen's chair and grinned down at her.

Gwen rose slowly and turned to face Harley. "Well, if it isn't the genius behind the success of *C.J.'s Journal.* We were just talking about you."

The mischievous gleam in Harley's eyes contradicted the serious expression on his face. "I thought I heard you telling C.J. how lucky you are to work for such a great guy."

Gwen glared and took a step toward Harley. "You're impossible. I don't know why I stay here."

He winked at C.J. "'Cause you know you're never gonna find another boss who takes such good care of you."

Gwen's face flushed. She headed toward the door. "I give up. See what you can do with him."

Harley watched until Gwen left the room, then smiled at C.J. "You gotta love that girl. Best researcher we've ever had here."

C.J. stood up, her gaze taking in Harley's white shirt with the gravy stain that had been there the day before. One thing about her producer—he never would make the top ten best-dressed list. "Maybe it's time to show your gratitude and ask Mr. Cunningham to give her a raise."

Harley held up his hands and backed away. "Whoa, there, girl. We gotta hit the top of the ratings first. Then we'll see who gets a raise."

She shook her head. "Gwen's right. You *are* impossible."

He winked and headed for the door. "Maybe. But I'm making you a household name around Oxford. Before I'm through with you, *C.J.'s Journal* will be the most listened to show in our area. And after that, who knows?" He flipped a little salute in her direction. "Catch you later. We need to talk about tonight's show. I have a feeling it's gonna be quite a broadcast."

For some reason his words, which on the surface seemed innocent enough, stirred the uneasiness she'd felt all morning. The stories she'd covered in the past few weeks flashed through her mind. Most of them were concerned with the dark side of life in Oxford, not what she'd intended when she began her program. For a moment she wished she'd never gotten caught up in the world of crime and drug dealers like Jimmy Carpenter. But there was no turning back.

A soft chime sounded from the direction of her computer. Another e-mail. She glanced at the screen and stared with

wide eyes at the sender's name—Fala. Her heart pounded at
the subject line. *Ready to play, C.J.?*

With shaking fingers she clicked the mouse and stared at
the message before her:

Four there are await your play,
One won't see the break of day,
From East to West they all will cry,
Who will be the first to die?
Fala

TWO

The words gyrated on the computer screen in rhythm with the drumbeat of C.J.'s heart. She grasped the edge of the desk, the message sending chills down her spine.

"Who will be the first to die?" she whispered.

If this was a joke, Fala had gone too far. She wrapped her shaking fingers around the phone handset to call Gwen. She hesitated, her eyes growing wider by the moment. What was it Harley had said? He had a feeling that tonight's show was going to be quite a broadcast.

Harley! Of course! She should have guessed.

This had to be one of his publicity stunts. He wanted to scare her into thinking someone was about to commit a crime in Oxford. If she went on the air and mentioned a menacing e-mail, they'd probably get a flood of calls.

Oh, the gall of that man to scare her so. With clenched fists she strode toward the office door and flung it open. Harley stood just down the hall talking to Michael Grayson, head of the sales department. "Harley! I need to see you now."

Michael pivoted and glared at her. "Wait your turn, C.J. He's mine right now."

C.J. stopped, her stomach roiling. This wasn't the first time she'd seen Harley and Michael arguing. Splotches of red covered Michael's craggy face, and a muscle twitched in his jaw.

Michael pushed his glasses up on his hawklike nose, the French cuffs of his Prada shirt slipping up to reveal a diamond-studded watch with an alligator band, and pointed his finger at Harley. "Now you listen to me, hotshot. If it wasn't for my staff, you wouldn't have any sponsors for *C.J.'s Journal,* or any of your other shows. You'd better watch your step or you'll find yourself without any financial backing, and you'll be off the air. Got it?"

Harley chuckled. "Sure, Mike. But from where I sit, your guys wouldn't have anything to sell if it wasn't for the interest my programs generate. Now get out there and do your job, and leave mine to me."

Harley turned away, but Michael grabbed his arm. "Just remember that you've been warned."

Harley pulled away from the restraining hand and swaggered down the hall toward C.J. "Now, doll. What can I do for you?"

C.J. couldn't take her eyes off Michael's angry face. He'd intimidated her since the first day she'd walked into the radio station, and now he was threatening her program. She couldn't let Harley's cocky attitude ruin what she'd worked so hard to achieve.

She glanced in Michael's direction. "Are you having trouble with the salespeople again?"

Harley waved his hand in dismissal. "It's nothing for you to worry about."

The e-mail flashed into her mind. "How could you do that to me?"

His eyebrows arched. "What are you talking about?"

"That e-mail! What are you trying to do—scare me to death?"

Harley studied her for a moment. "I don't know what you're talking about."

She grabbed his arm, pulled him inside her office and propelled him to her desk chair. She pointed a shaking finger at the computer screen. "This is what I'm talking about."

Harley leaned forward as he read the e-mail. After a few moments, he chuckled. "Do you think I sent this?"

She crossed her arms. "Yes."

"Well, I didn't. Don't have any idea who did, but I kinda like it."

The man never ceased to amaze her. "What?"

"Yeah. This means you've struck a nerve somewhere, and this lunatic wants to make you squirm a little. Congratulations. This is the kind of stuff that can keep listeners tuning in."

"Harley, you're impossible. I don't want to attract crazy people."

"This guy probably just wants some attention. Nobody's gonna talk about a crime before they commit it." He tilted his head as if in thought. A slow smile pulled at his lips. "Of course, we could run with this tonight and see if the mysterious e-mailer will call in to talk."

C.J. backed away from him, her head shaking back and forth. "Don't you even suggest it, Harley. I'm not about to encourage people like this."

"Aw, C.J. C'mon. It could be…"

"No!"

"But…"

She grabbed her purse from the desk. "I'll be out of here in two minutes if you don't go along with me on this."

Harley was a head shorter than she was, but his determination could make her resolve slip. He'd done it before. But not this time. Her phone rang, breaking the silence between them. She straightened her shoulders and ignored it, her gaze never wavering from his.

Finally, he grinned and stuck his hands in his pockets. "Okay, have it your way. But I think it's a mistake."

She didn't say anything, and after a few moments he headed toward the door. When he'd disappeared down the hall, she sank down in her desk chair and read the message again. Was somebody really about to die?

If this was the kind of people who were tuning in to her program, maybe the talk show wasn't worth it. But then that would mean that Mitch had been right all along. With a groan she closed the e-mail program and sat there, staring at the blank screen.

The words, no longer visible on the screen, appeared in her mind as if they'd been seared into her innermost thoughts. She crossed her arms and hugged her body to stop the trembling that swept through her. If the message was to be believed, four people were walking around Oxford unaware that death was stalking them. She had no idea who they were or why she had been chosen to rescue them from the evil they were about to encounter.

"If only I could warn them," she whispered.

Mitch didn't know what made him take the long route to work and then turn down the street where C.J. lived. He knew he wouldn't see her. By this time of morning, she'd already been at the radio station for hours. Maybe it was a leftover habit from picking her up to go out, or it could be that he just wanted to feel close to her again. At times during the last month he'd thought he would go out of his mind from wanting to see her, talk to her or just sit quietly and hold her hand.

He could still envision her as she was two years ago when she'd interviewed him about a murder in Oxford. He'd been surprised when she informed him that she remembered him from college. He had no recollection of her, but in later weeks he couldn't understand how he'd missed out on someone so special.

For him no other woman would ever measure up to C.J. She was beautiful with her long, brown hair and hazel eyes, but that was only part of the attraction he felt toward her.

Behind her flashing eyes was an intelligence he felt he could never quite match. And because she never tried to appear superior to anyone, it only increased the magnetism she radiated.

When she broke the engagement, it had caught him completely off guard. He'd known she was under a lot of stress getting the new show started. They'd disagreed about her doing it, just as they had disagreed about her refusal to acknowledge any need for God in her life. The arguments had never gotten heated, or at least he hadn't thought so.

Patrolling the streets of Oxford for several years before being promoted to detective had taught him how dangerous situations could become in the blink of an eye. It had also reinforced his belief that he couldn't get through the day without the peace that came from knowing God watched over him. He wanted C.J. to know that love, too.

Mitch drove down the street and pulled to a stop in front of C.J.'s house. He sat there thinking about all the times she'd come running out to meet him. Her eyes would light up, and his heart would beat a little faster at how right it felt for them to be together. All that changed when she gave the ring back.

A tap at the window startled him, and he jumped in surprise. He turned to see Mary Warren, C.J.'s next-door neighbor, standing beside him. He smiled and rolled the window down. "Good morning, Mary. I didn't see you."

The elderly lady smiled. "I've been walking Otto and saw your car. I wanted to say hello."

At the mention of her schnauzer, the dog jumped up on the side of the car. Mary pulled on the leash and took a step back. "Otto, get down."

Otto's paws slid downward, and Mitch cringed at the sound of Otto's nails scraping on metal. He dreaded seeing the scratch on his new paint job. Mary pulled Otto back, but he tugged hard on the leash to reach the car. C.J. and Mitch had often laughed that Otto had Mary trained well.

Mitch opened the door and stepped out in an effort to distract Otto from jumping up again. He knelt down and patted the dog. "How are you today, boy?"

Mary beamed at Mitch as he rose. "Otto has always liked you."

Mitch smiled. "How have you been?"

Mary's faded blue eyes stared at Mitch. The jogging suit she wore swallowed her small body. She'd lost weight in the last few weeks. Every time he saw Mary, he wondered how much longer she could live alone. Her mind wasn't as sharp as it had been a year ago, but that didn't distract from what she saw as her mission in life.

Ever since Mary's husband had died, she'd been obsessed with what she saw as the rising crime rate in Oxford. She'd become so concerned that she had appointed herself as a neighborhood watchdog to keep an eye out for danger. Every time he saw Mary, she had another incident to report to him.

Mary glanced over her shoulder toward the street. "All right, I guess. But I wanted to tell you about the woman I saw this morning sitting across the street in a strange car."

"Maybe she was visiting someone." Mitch wondered how many times Mary had approached him with her worries.

Mary shook her head. "I don't think so. She was sitting there when I left for my walk with Otto, and she hadn't left forty-five minutes later when we came back. I watched her after I went in the house. She drove off about fifteen minutes later when C.J. did. In fact, she followed C.J."

An uneasy feeling welled up in Mitch. "What did the car look like, Mary?"

She reached in her pocket and pulled out a small notebook. "I don't know anything about cars. All I know is that it was big and black. But I wrote down the license plate number." She tore the paper from the pad and held it out to him. "You know I never go anywhere without my notebook."

Mitch smiled, took the paper and put his arm around Mary's shoulders. "I'm sure it was very innocent. But if it'll make you feel better, I'll check on it. Now you go on home, and don't worry."

She patted his arm and stared at him for a moment. "You're a good boy, Mitch."

He climbed back in his car as Mary shuffled toward her house with Otto in tow. Mitch stared at the number in Mary's shaky handwriting before he pulled his cell phone from his pocket and speed-dialed the police department's number.

With the first ring, the dispatcher answered. "Oxford Police Department."

"Jennie, this is Mitch Harmon. I need you to run a license plate for me."

"Sure, Mitch."

He read the numbers and waited for her computer search. Within seconds she was back on the phone.

"Got it, Mitch."

"Who's the car registered to?"

"None other than Jimmy Carpenter."

The words hit Mitch like a punch in the stomach. "Thanks, Jennie."

He closed the phone and sat lost in thought. Why was a car belonging to the drug lord of Oxford sitting across the street from C.J.'s house and following her? Maybe that radio show was becoming even more dangerous than he thought.

The hands on the wall clock pointed to 3:45 p.m. C.J. sat in the broadcast area, her palms damp with sweat. She stared through the window into the adjacent room where Harley busied himself checking the control board before airtime. Just a few more minutes and she'd be transmitting live.

Four to 7:00 p.m.—the most coveted segment of afternoon drive time. She still had to pinch herself to believe that the station had given it to her. But it seemed to be paying off. Her ratings were climbing every week. She just hoped Harley's disagreement with Michael Grayson didn't do anything to jeopardize the program.

She pulled the microphone closer to her mouth and reached up to check the earphones again. In the next room Harley mouthed the countdown, his fingers cueing her to the seconds left before broadcast. With a grin he pointed to her.

C.J. took a deep breath and leaned closer to the console. "Good afternoon, and welcome to *C.J.'s Journal.* You're listening to WLMT-FM in Oxford, on the air with C.J. Tanner. It's good to be back among friends. No matter where you are, at home or driving from work, loosen that tie, settle back and get ready to spend the next three hours chatting with me about life in Oxford. Get your questions and comments ready and call me at 555-WLMT—that's the number. But while those calls are coming in, we're going to take a few minutes to recognize our sponsor. I'll be back right after this message."

She clicked off and glanced to her left at the call screener. The calls, first routed to Harley, were approved before they were put through to the broadcast booth. The caller ID on the monitor displayed the incoming phone numbers, and she watched as he lined them up for her. She always felt a moment of apprehension before the first question. Once into the broadcast, she relaxed, letting the callers voice their concerns and responding to them in a lively give-and-take.

All too soon the commercial ended. Harley was counting down again. She scanned the caller screen and frowned: the display read *private number.* They had agreed when the show went on the air that all callers had to be identified. Why was Harley putting this one through?

She looked at Harley and shook her head, but he motioned for her to take the call.

Frowning, she spoke into the microphone. "This is C.J. What's on your mind tonight?"

A soft chuckle sounded on the other end of the line, and a voice purred into her ear. "My name is Fala. I thought we might tell your listeners about our game."

Cold fear washed over her, and she fumbled to bring the mic closer. "I'm sorry. I don't think I understand."

"Come on, C.J. You know what I mean. I sent you a riddle this morning. Have you solved it yet?"

The voice held a wheedling tone and maybe a Southern drawl. But one thing she was certain of—she was talking to Fala.

From the next room Harley grinned at her. C.J. motioned to him to cut the call, but he shook his head. "If you don't have something to discuss, then I'm going to take the next caller."

"But I want everybody to know about our little game. I sent a riddle telling you I'm going to kill somebody. The only way to stop me is for you to solve it."

C.J. glared at Harley who appeared to be enjoying every word of the exchange. "Okay, I've heard enough. I don't appreciate practical jokes."

A long sigh came over the line. "I assure you this is no joke. Maybe you don't understand. Someone is about to die, and only you can save them."

She swallowed and struggled to speak. "Wh-who's going to d-die?"

Fala's exasperated sigh sent chills down C.J.'s spine. "You disappoint me, C.J. Instead of trying to figure out the riddle, you expect me to tell you the answer. That's against the rules. If you want to win, you have to do it on your own."

She sat silent, her mind whirling, but Harley motioned for her to keep the caller talking. No dead air—one of his cardinal rules.

She straightened in her chair and tried again. "Okay, Fala— if that's your real name—tell me more about this game you're playing that's going to end in someone's death. Surely you don't expect me to believe that, do you?"

A shrill laugh echoed in C.J.'s ear. "You'd better believe it. I'm not afraid to kill."

C.J.'s. shaking fingers clutched the edge of the console. "But why would you do such a horrible thing?"

"Maybe it's because of the look in their eyes."

"What do you mean?"

There was a moment of hesitation. "Because they never expect it. And when they realize what's happening, it's too late."

This was escalating into a horrible nightmare. Mitch's warning flashed into her mind, but she pushed it aside. "Fala, you can't be serious."

The laughter increased. "Oh, but I am. I'm about to kill someone, somewhere in Oxford, and the only way you can stop me is to figure out the riddle. If you haven't done it yet, you're not going to. So this one's for you, C.J."

The phone clicked in her ear, leaving behind a dead silence that chilled her blood and sent goose bumps flying over her flesh. Harley's clenched fist shot into the air, and he mouthed a big "All right" as the board lit up with calls.

C.J. covered her face with her hands and shook. Never in her life had she heard such hatred in a voice. Could Fala be telling the truth? Was someone about to die?

All she could do was hope it was someone playing a joke on her. But something told her that Fala meant every word he said.

When C.J. switched the last caller off, she stormed out of the broadcast booth. Harley, his face filled with satisfaction, grinned at her. "Some night, huh? Your ratings ought to go through the roof tomorrow."

"Harley," she yelled, "how could you let that person stay on the line?"

He reached out toward her, but she swatted his hand away. His face creased into the little boy look she'd come to recognize as his way of saying I-want-my-way. "Now, C.J., you have to expect these crazies to come out of the woodwork every once in a while. You gotta use them to build your audience appeal. That's all I was doing."

"But he said he was going to kill somebody!"

"Aw, don't pay any attention to that," he purred. "Whoever it was just wanted fifteen minutes of fame, and I gave it to him. You'll never hear from Fala again."

C.J. crossed her arms and shook her head. "You don't know that."

Harley began to shut the console off. "Come on. The satellite programming has taken over. Let's go home. I'll walk you to your car."

C.J. hugged her arms around her body and shivered. By this time it would be dark outside, and she didn't want to walk into that parking lot alone. "Okay, let me get my coat, and we'll go."

Walking back to her office, she looked over her shoulder with each step. She couldn't shake the feeling that something evil had invaded WLMT.

The wooded area across from WLMT provided the perfect place to observe the radio station. Three of the tall letters on the flat roof burned this evening and cast an outline of the boxlike, two-story brick building against the night sky. Office lights on the second floor went out. Harley and C.J. must be getting ready to leave. Fala pulled the coat pocket open and dropped the cell phone into it.

C.J. had been scared all right. It was evident in the way her voice trembled. Would she walk to her car alone? No, she'd be afraid that Fala would be waiting.

I'm close, C.J. Can you see me?

The door to the station opened and Harley Martin escorted C.J. to her car. She got in, rolled the window down and spoke to him. He nodded and walked around the car, testing the locks on each door. When he'd finished, he waved, and jogged back to his truck. C.J. waited until he pulled up behind her before she drove into the street.

"Oh, C.J., you're so predictable. That's what makes you such an easy target," Fala muttered.

With excitement growing at what lay ahead, Fala turned and strode back through the trees to the car on the other side of the woods. Moonlight drifted through the bare branches. A cat chewed on the carcass of a dead bird at the end of the path. A well-placed kick sent the feline darting away.

Fala's gloved hand picked up the bird's lifeless form and caressed it. The smell of death drifted upward. It radiated through his every pore and set his every sense on fire.

The hand holding the bird's body shot toward the sky. "Let the game begin!"

THREE

5:00 a.m.

The bedside clock glowed in the early morning darkness. C.J. moaned and pounded her pillow into shape once more. Last night, when she had arrived home and checked her computer, she saw that another e-mail had awaited her. With shaking fingers she opened the message and read it, her eyes growing wider with each word.

You didn't guess, my first move's through,
Someone now is blaming you.
You should have stopped my fun-filled spree,
Death surrounds you, wait and see.
Fala

Chilled by the reminder of a maniacal laugh and a sinister message, she had cowered underneath the covers.

With a groan, she sat up in bed. She couldn't sleep anymore because of her worry about Fala's e-mail, so she decided to go for a morning run to distract herself.

A few minutes later she walked into the kitchen. Dressed in sweats, her key ring hanging from her wrist, she adjusted the band covering her ears and headed into the cold. Very few lights burned in the neighborhood houses on the street. How she envied those sleeping peacefully in their beds.

She approached the intersection at the end of the street, the slap of her tennis shoes on the pavement beating out a steady rhythm. She had laid out the square that composed her two-mile route when she first moved in the neighborhood, and it never varied. Left from her driveway, right on Crump Avenue, right on Knight's Way, right on Bellevue and finally back onto Lansdowne. She always breathed a sigh of relief when she made that last turn onto her street and jogged into her driveway.

There were never many vehicles on the roads this time of morning. She liked it that way—alone with her thoughts, no sounds except the panting of her breath and her shoes hitting the asphalt. A car approached from the rear, causing her to glance backward. A black SUV moved toward her, its engine purring. She jogged to the edge of the street to let it pass, but it stayed behind her. Her chest tightened. In the early morning light it was impossible to tell for sure, but it looked like the car she'd spotted across from her house the day before.

Her heart pounded, and she picked up her pace. The vehicle maintained its slow speed. Taking a deep breath, she surged forward. The car sped up, but didn't pass. Now she ran faster, the SUV's engine humming in her ears. Certain that she was being pursued, she lengthened her strides until the muscles in her thighs screamed in pain and her lungs burned. The car crept behind her like a giant shadow, waiting to pounce.

Ahead she could see the turn onto her street, and she willed her legs to move even faster. As she turned onto Lansdowne, the newspaper delivery van rumbled toward her. With a roar, the SUV shot past her and disappeared down the street.

Panting for breath, C.J. stopped and leaned over, her hands propped on her knees. She gulped mouthfuls of air. The deliveryman paused to wave before flinging a newspaper onto a driveway. C.J. sank down on the curb and smiled in relief.

Had she really been followed or had her imagination run away with her? After a few minutes, she rose and trotted toward home. As she passed Mary's house, she slowed and let her gaze travel over the brick structure. Something was out of place.

She stopped in her driveway and stared at the dark house. With a shrug she headed to her front door. Her sleep-deprived brain must be conjuring up problems where there were none.

Thirty minutes later, fresh from the shower and wearing jeans and a sweatshirt, she stepped into the kitchen. She poured herself a cup of coffee and remembered that she hadn't yet brought in the newspaper. Hurrying out the front door into the driveway, she scooped up the paper, then stopped and stared at Mary Warren's house. What was different this morning?

Her eyes widened. The closed living-room drapes. She'd never seen that before. Mary, who retired early every evening, was always up by this time, and she never drew the curtains in her living room. The newspaper dropped from her hand. She ran across the yard and stopped at Mary's front door.

The unlocked storm door opened with her touch, and she pounded on the wooden front door. "Mary! Mary!"

From somewhere inside, Otto howled. C.J. cupped her hands around her eyes and leaned close to the small glass pane in the door. She looked into the dark, but could detect no movement. Otto wailed again.

She backed away, her legs shaking. Maybe Mary was sick or hurt. She raced across the yard and rushed into her house. Running to the bedroom, she grabbed the key ring she'd tossed on the dresser before showering. Months ago Mary had insisted that C.J. take a key to her house. It made her feel better to know that a trusted neighbor could get in if there were ever an emergency.

She ran out the back door and toward the gate in the fence that separated their yards, leaped onto the back porch, and pounded her fist against the door. "Mary! Let me in."

Inside, Otto's howl pierced the air, and he pawed at the door.

The keys jingled against each other as C.J. tried to jam the key in the lock. After several attempts, her shaking fingers finally inserted the key and turned it. Otto jumped up on her leg the moment she stepped inside.

She patted his head and stepped into the dark kitchen. An ominous silence hovered in the air. She stopped just inside the door and switched the kitchen light on. Otto ran to the door to the den and hesitated. He looked back as if inviting her to follow, then dashed from the room.

A strange smell assaulted her nose. She inched toward the den.

"M-Mary!"

Her voice echoed through the house.

Another step. "Mary, are you all right?"

The tapping of Otto's paws on the hardwood of the den caused her to halt. He ran through the door and whined. "Where's your mama, Otto? In her bedroom?"

C.J. switched on the den light and walked toward the dark hallway on the other side that led to the bedrooms. Otto ran ahead of her and stopped at Mary's closed bedroom door.

She tapped on the door. "Mary, are you in there?"

As she pushed the door open, Otto wiggled past and disappeared into the bedroom. The rusty scent poured from the room and overwhelmed her. She staggered backward into the hall.

Otto rushed back to her, raised his head and howled before he leaned forward and nuzzled her leg, the red stain on his nose smearing her jeans. What was it? She reached down, touched his nose, and studied her fingertips. With a strangled cry she fell against the wall and stood there, her eyes transfixed on the bedroom door.

Slowly, she pushed the door open wide. Cold sweat popped out on her forehead. She swallowed and groped the wall for the light switch. The chandelier illuminated the room the moment she turned it on.

C.J. pressed her hand to her mouth to suppress the scream that welled up from the depths of her soul. The bedroom that Mary had so lovingly decorated looked like a chamber of horrors. Red stains soaked the carpet around the bed where Mary's lifeless body lay. Blood covered the once-white sheets and comforter.

But that wasn't the worst. On the walls red handprints, arranged much like a kindergarten fingerpaint project, covered the white sheetrock.

"No-o-o."

Early mornings had always been Mitch's favorite part of the day—a time when he could reflect on God's promises. This morning, though, he couldn't turn past the page in his Bible with the passage he'd underlined a month ago when C.J. broke their engagement.

Do not be yoked together with unbelievers.

How many times had he read that in the past few weeks? He'd known what the Bible said. Even Pastor Donald had cautioned him when he started dating C.J., but he thought he could change her. He should have listened and backed away before he fell in love. Now he was suffering the consequences.

His gaze drifted downward. *What does a believer have in common with an unbeliever?*

The words tore at Mitch's soul, and he bowed his head. "Oh, Lord," he prayed, "Forgive me for thinking I was smart enough to escape being hurt by disobeying your teachings. I thought I could bring her to You, but I failed. Please give me the strength to let her go now, Father, but I beg You not to give up on her."

He sat with his head bowed for several minutes before he glanced out the window at the first light of day beginning to break, then at his wristwatch—6:30 a.m. He still had a few hours before he needed to check in at the station.

He drained the rest of the coffee and stood up to pour himself another cup. His cell phone rang, always a cause for concern this early in the morning. The station's number flashed on the caller ID.

"Hello."

"Mitch, this is Jennie at dispatch. Just got a call reporting a murder. First responders are already there, but the chief thinks you and Myra need to get over there right away."

Mitch hurried toward the bedroom, the phone pressed to his ear. "Have you called Myra?"

"No, but I will."

"Good." Mitch reached for his wallet on the dresser and stuffed it in his pants pocket. "What's the address?"

Jennie took a deep breath. "417 Lansdowne Drive."

His fingers tightened around the gun he'd just picked up and he felt his heart constrict. "What did you say?"

"C.J. called in the report. She just found her neighbor Mary Warren murdered."

He lowered the gun back to the dresser top and swallowed. "Mary? Murdered?"

"I'm sorry, Mitch. I know you were fond of Mary. From what C.J. said, it's really bad."

He pressed his hand to his forehead. "Is C.J. all right?"

"She's pretty upset. She was practically hysterical when she called."

Mitch shook his head, grabbed the gun again and straightened his shoulders. No time to be upset. He had a job to do. "Call Myra and tell her to meet me there. I'm on my way."

He flipped the cell phone closed and headed for the door, his thoughts whirling. The memory of Mary's concern yesterday flashed through his mind.

Guilt pierced his soul. He'd thought about checking on Mary the night before. A call had come in just as he was leaving work, and he'd been tied up until late. When he finished, he'd thought C.J. might be home from the station. He needed to stay away from her, and he wasn't sure he'd be able to do that if he saw her lights on. So he'd gone back to his apartment, warmed up some pizza and watched a ball game until it was time for bed.

Suppose he had gone to Mary's. Could he have saved her life? He stopped beside his car and pounded his fist on the roof. He would never know the answer to that question, but he knew it would weigh on him for a long time.

C.J. stared out the window over Mary's kitchen sink. Otto lay on the back porch, his head resting on his outstretched paws. His cries of distress had now dissolved into soft whines.

She slid into a chair at the table and sat there, staring into space, her hands folded on the tabletop in front of her. Hushed voices drifted from the living room. From time to time the front door opened and closed, and new voices joined those already in the house. Every few minutes another officer, his face pale, would appear in the hallway outside the kitchen, lean against the wall and offer a weak smile in her direction.

Mitch had often told her he had never become immune to the horrors one human being could inflict on another. She realized that some of these men hadn't, either, although they appeared to be seasoned veterans. She could understand their need to step away from this horrible crime scene for a minute.

Her stomach heaved, and she ran to the sink. She leaned over until the sickness passed, then turned the water on full force and washed up.

A hand touched her shoulder. She screamed and whirled around. Mitch stood behind her, his eyes filled with concern. She collapsed against the side of the sink and stood there, staring at him. With a cry, she threw her arms around him and pressed her cheek against his chest. His arms encircled her and rocked her back and forth.

It felt good to be in his arms. Now that he'd arrived, everything would be all right. "Oh, Mitch, I'm so glad you're here."

After a few moments she pulled away and gazed up at him. His jaw twitched. "Are you okay?"

Her stomach rumbled again, and she pressed her palms against it. "Did you see her? Why would anybody do that?"

He raked his hand through his hair. "I don't know. I've never seen anything like it."

She could barely stand to ask the next question, but she had to know. "Did the killer dip his hands in her blood and then touch the walls?"

"Yes."

"Then you can get fingerprints, right?"

"It looks like he may have worn some kind of gloves."

C.J. dropped into the chair again, and the key ring in her pocket rattled. She touched the bulge of keys, her eyes growing wide. "The house was locked. I had to use my key to get in. How did the killer leave all the doors bolted?"

"We don't know, but we're just beginning our investigation." He paused a moment, then eased into the chair next to her. He reached out and covered her hand with his. "Which brings me to what I have to do next. We need to ask you some questions."

"We?"

"Myra and I."

Of course. Mitch didn't check out any crime scene without his partner.

Myra walked into the room, sat in the chair across from C.J. and pulled a notepad from her pocket. Her fingers flipped the pages until she found a blank one. A tiny bead of perspiration slid down the side of Myra's face, and she swallowed several times before she looked up. "I can understand how upset you are. We'll make this as brief as possible."

"Thank you, Myra."

C.J. glanced from Myra's pale features to Mitch, whose fingers still clutched hers. Even if they were trained police officers, C.J. realized that the murder scene in the next room had left both of them shaken.

Mitch cleared his throat. "Okay, can you tell us what made you come over here this morning?"

Where to begin? With the e-mails and the call or noticing the closed drapes?

"Did you hear my show last night?"

Mitch shook his head. "I was on a call until late. Why?"

"Because, because…" Her lips trembled. She glanced around the kitchen where she'd visited with Mary many times. Otto's leash hung on a peg at the backdoor. The teakettle sat on the stove. She and Mary had shared many cups of tea together, but they never would again. C.J. covered her face with her hands. "Because it's my fault Mary is dead," she wailed.

Mitch touched her arm. "What are you talking about?"

Tears squeezed between her fingers that still covered her eyes. "I should have solved the riddle."

Mitch's chair scraped on the floor as he pushed back from the table. He reached for a paper towel at the sink and wedged it into her hand. "Here."

She wiped at her eyes and blew her nose. "Thanks."

Mitch sank back down in his chair and cleared his throat. "What's this about a riddle?"

She twisted the paper towel between her fingers. "Harley said nobody would admit they were going to commit a crime, but I thought Fala really meant it."

Mitch and Myra exchanged glances. "Fala?" he said.

The paper towel was now reduced to shreds in her hand. "Mary was just the first. The riddle said there would be four murders. And I don't know who they are." She jumped up and stared down at Mitch. "You've got to stop Fala!"

Mitch rose to stand beside her and put his arm around her shoulders. "You're not making any sense, C.J.. Who is Fala, and what does that have to do with Mary's murder?"

C.J. slumped against him, and he eased her back into her chair before sitting beside her. She took a deep breath, straightened in her seat and thought back to the events of the morning before. "It all began yesterday…"

Concentrating on the first e-mail and everything that happened afterward, she related each message and the call from Fala. When she'd finished, she looked to Mitch, then Myra. "In the last message Fala said the first move had been made. Mary must have already been dead by the time I received that e-mail."

As C.J. finished speaking, Myra made another notation in her notebook. "We'll need copies of those messages."

C.J. nodded. "I deleted the first one, but I don't think I've emptied the trash yet. Maybe I can retrieve it."

Mitch stood up. "Good. Why don't we go over to your house and do that right now?" He glanced at Myra. "I'll go with C.J. if you'll finish up here."

Myra scribbled one last word in the notebook and closed it. "Sure. No problem."

"Detectives, could I see you for a moment?" They all turned to stare in the direction of the deep voice. A young man, dressed in jeans and a T-shirt with latex gloves on, stood in the doorway. Mitch and Myra stepped over to him.

Mitch's broad shoulders blocked C.J.'s view of the man. "Did you find something, Jeff?"

"Yes, sir. We found a blond hair in the victim's hand."

Mitch and Myra seemed unaware that C.J. now stood directly behind them.

Myra leaned toward Mitch. "Interesting. Maybe the killer left a calling card."

"Don't know about that," the man said. "That'll be for you guys to decide. Just wanted you to know."

"Thanks," Mitch said.

C.J. started to step back, but Mitch turned before she could and plowed into her. "Sorry. Didn't know you were right behind me. Ready to go get those e-mails?"

Just then a howl rose from the back porch. Tears welled in C.J.'s eyes again. "Otto. What's going to happen to him?"

Mitch shook his head. "I don't know. We'll send for the Humane Society. They'll take care of him until they can find him a home."

C.J. turned toward the back door. "I want to go out through the backyard so I can say goodbye to him."

She paused before stepping outside and glanced in the direction of the bedroom. Biting her lip, she said a silent farewell to her friend. She wished she could tell Mary how sorry she was for not solving the riddle, but that was impossible. The only thing she could do now was try to stop Fala before three more people died.

FOUR

As Mitch waited for C.J. to release Otto, he shivered in the cold morning air, but it was more than just the temperature that chilled him today. A cold-blooded murderer had struck in a vicious way, killing a beloved friend and terrifying the woman he loved. If C.J. were right, there might be additional victims. In his years on the force, he hadn't seen anything to compare with Mary's bedroom. Overkill. That was the only word to describe it.

The crime scene puzzled him. Surely Otto had barked when the killer entered the house, but Mary's body lay in bed as if she hadn't been alerted. And how did the killer get into a locked house with no apparent forced entry? Had they overlooked something in their initial sweep through the rooms? He'd go back after he printed a copy of the e-mails and take another look around. By the time he completed this investigation, he'd probably be familiar with every nook and cranny of Mary's house.

C.J. rose from petting Otto and touched Mitch's arm. "I'm ready now."

Police cars, their blue lights flashing in the early-morning gloom, lined the street in front of the house. Several grim-faced officers silently roped off the house with crime scene tape. A cluster of neighbors stood nearby, watching the proceedings.

"Mitch. C.J." The voice came from the direction of the neighbors gathered near the edge of C.J.'s front yard. Adam Connor emerged from the crowd and ran toward the fence. Disbelief lined his face. "One of the ladies from across the street told me Mary is dead. Is that true?"

Mitch nodded. "I'm afraid so."

Adam's fingers grasped the top of the fence, and he shifted his gaze from one to the other, his mouth open. "I-I can't believe this." He glanced back at the officers who'd just completed roping off the house. "Mitch, that's crime scene tape. What's going on here?"

"Mary was murdered."

Adam gasped, his hands tightening on the fence. "Murdered? Not Mary." His eyes grew wide. "When?"

"Apparently last night." The scene in the bedroom flashed into Mitch's mind, and he swallowed. "C.J. found the body."

Adam turned to stare at her. "Oh, C.J., how awful. Are you all right?"

She nodded. "I think so. I just can't get that sight out of my mind."

Adam leaned against the fence. "I was on my way to the gym when I saw the activity out here, but that can wait. You want me to come in and stay with you a while?"

"I think that's a good idea, Adam," Mitch said. "She's still pretty shaken up and doesn't need to be alone."

"I'll do anything I can to help. Maybe we need to call Gwen to come over, too."

Mitch nodded. "We'll go in through the back and let you in the front door."

Adam raked his hand through his hair. "Mary murdered. I can't believe it. I just talked to her yesterday."

"Me, too." The vision of Mary and Otto walking up and down the street popped into Mitch's head. No longer would the two patrol the neighborhood on their self-appointed rounds to keep a watch for evil. Instead it had entered her house when she'd least expected it and left a grisly murder in its wake. Mary's crime-fighting days might be over, but his weren't. Mitch didn't intend for this to become a cold case. He wouldn't rest until Mary's killer was brought to justice.

C.J. and Mitch stepped onto the back porch, and she grasped the knob of the back door. It turned in her fingers, but she jerked her hand away. She'd left her back door unlocked when she ran to Mary's. Someone could have been watching. The murderer could be inside just waiting for her to come home.

"What's wrong?" Mitch said from behind her.

She stumbled backward. "I left the door unlocked. What if someone's inside?"

He grabbed her hand. "Don't worry. Whoever killed Mary is long gone."

"But what if they're not?"

He pulled the gun from his belt. "If it'll make you feel better, I'll search the house before you go in."

"Thanks. I'd appreciate that."

She moved out of the way and let Mitch slip into the kitchen. Minutes passed before he reappeared, Adam right behind him. "All clear. Come on inside."

She shuffled into the kitchen, her face burning. "I'm sorry."

Adam walked around Mitch and wrapped his arms around her. "There's nothing for you to be sorry about."

She hugged him and looked over his shoulder toward Mitch, their eyes locking. It was Mitch's arms she wanted around her. He should be the one comforting her, but today he was the professional police investigator.

Mitch inclined his head toward the den. "C.J.?"

Adam turned to face him. "What is it?"

C.J. pulled away and pushed her hair behind her ears. "I have to get some e-mails off my computer for Mitch."

"The ones you got yesterday at work?"

A surprised look flashed on Mitch's face. "How did you know about that?"

"Gwen told me last night at dinner. She said you were upset about them, but Harley didn't think they meant anything."

C.J. closed her eyes and massaged her temples. "That's what I thought, too, until the mysterious Fala called my show and then sent another message."

Adam sucked in his breath. "Gwen didn't tell me about that."

"She didn't know. It happened after she'd left for the day."

Mitch checked his watch. "I really need to get back over to Mary's."

"I'll print out those e-mails now," she said, heading toward the den. She rubbed her hands on her pants. "Then I think I'll shower again before I go to work."

Mitch reached out and stopped her. "Whoa, there. You don't need to go to work. Why don't you take the day off?"

"I can't do that. I have a broadcast to do."

Mitch waved his hand in dismissal. "Cancel it, or let Harley do it. You don't need to go anywhere until we find out about whoever's sending you these threatening messages."

"What should I do? Hide in my house? No, thanks. Fala isn't going to get in the way of my show or my life."

He leaned toward her, gritting his teeth. "Don't be so hard-headed. Your show isn't worth the risk."

Mitch might have appeared concerned about her this morning, but his words told her nothing had changed between them. "Not to you. You've certainly made that clear from the beginning, but it is to me."

Mitch raked his hand through his hair. "Sometimes you…"

Adam stepped up beside them and placed a hand on each

one's shoulder. "Hey, guys, stop it. You're both upset, but you don't need to argue. We've lost a great friend." He paused, blinked back tears and took a deep breath. "I'll tell you what. You two get the e-mails, and I'll cook breakfast. Then we'll all sit down and try to cope with what's happened."

Mitch's shoulders sagged. "You and C.J. can eat. I'll grab something later on."

Adam frowned. "C'mon, Mitch. You've got to eat."

"Sorry, I can't. The chief will be waiting at the station for me."

Adam nodded. "Then I'll call Gwen to come over. C.J. can ride to work with her after breakfast. How's that?"

She couldn't believe it. They were standing here talking about her as if she weren't capable of making her own decisions. "You don't have to ask Mitch, Adam," she said. "I'll decide how I'll go to work."

Mitch's eyes narrowed, and he let out a long breath. "Fine. I suppose I can't stop you from what you're bound and determined to do. Just give me the e-mails, and I'll get out of your way."

Without a word she turned and led the way into the den. Adam's voice drifted from the kitchen. She knew he'd dialed Gwen. "This is Adam. Something terrible has happened." His voice dissolved into choking sobs. "Can you come to C.J.'s house?"

Dreading to open her e-mails, C.J. eased into her desk chair and turned on the computer. As she waited for it to boot, she closed her eyes in an effort to forget the horrible scene in Mary's bedroom. She could only imagine the message Fala might have left to torment her for not saving her friend's life.

Finally she opened her eyes, held her breath and clicked. No new message from Fala in her inbox. Cold fear replaced the short-lived relief that flooded her body.

With Mary dead, three victims remained. Only Fala knew their names and the times of their deaths.

Who would be next?

The smells from the kitchen had teased her nose while she printed the e-mails for Mitch, and she'd hoped he would change his mind about staying. Instead, he'd scooped up the papers from the printer tray and headed back to Mary's without so much as a goodbye.

Gwen dropped the piece of toast she'd been nibbling onto her plate. "I didn't know you were such a good cook, Adam. Maybe I need to take lessons from you."

He reached across the table and covered her hand with his. "Anytime, lovely lady. You know I'm at your service."

C.J. smiled at the two of them. It was evident the attraction they'd felt when she introduced them a few months ago was blossoming into something deeper. She wiped her hands on her napkin and stared at the scrambled eggs in front of her. Adam had done a great job with the meal, but she couldn't bring herself to eat. She lifted her fork and traced the flower pattern on the edge of the plate with the tines.

"C.J.?" Gwen's voice caught her attention.

"Yes?"

"If you're finished, Adam and I will clean up while you get dressed."

She pushed back from the table and stood. "Thanks for being here, you two. It means a lot to have such good friends."

Gwen rose and put her arm around C.J.'s shoulder. "We're glad to help."

Adam nodded. "Gwen's right. We love you, and we'll do anything we can for you."

Fighting back tears, C.J. rushed toward the bedroom. Maybe a hot shower would make her feel better.

Thirty minutes later her reflection gazed at her from the dresser mirror. The dark circles under her eyes refused to disappear, even with a thick layer of makeup. She fluffed her hair one more time. What did it matter how she looked anymore? Who was there to care? Her audience would never know.

The doorbell rang. Maybe Adam or Gwen would get it. She listened for a moment until she heard the front door open and Adam's voice. The storm door closed, and she supposed he had stepped outside.

Picking up her purse and coat, she headed toward the living room. She pulled the curtain back at the front window and looked out. Adam and Mitch stood on the sidewalk in front of the house talking. Adam nodded in agreement before Mitch turned and strode to his unmarked police car. When he pulled away from the curb, Myra followed. C.J. let the curtains fall back into place and watched Adam reenter the house.

"There you are," he said. "Gwen's waiting for you in the kitchen."

She pulled her coat on and busied herself with the buttons. "What did Mitch want?"

A tiny frown creased Adam's forehead. "He asked me to keep an eye on you for him."

C.J. lifted her head and sniffed. "Does he think I need a keeper?"

He waved his hand in dismissal. "Of course not. He's just concerned."

She reached into her coat pocket and drew out her gloves. "Well, he could have come in and said goodbye."

"C.J., give the poor guy a break. You were the one who broke the engagement. If you'd meet him halfway, maybe the two of you could work out your problems." Adam stopped, and she knew he wanted her to say something. When she didn't, he turned away. "Never mind. I'll tell Gwen you're ready to go."

Adam's words made sense. She'd sent Mitch away, and there was no going back. It was too late for them, and now it was too late for Mary. She swiped at the dampness on her face as the words of the riddle ran through her mind. It was as much a mystery to her now as it had been when she first saw it.

She clenched her fists. Why couldn't she figure out the hidden meaning in Fala's message? She could have saved Mary if she had. Now she had to live with a terrible truth—Mary's death was her fault.

FIVE

C.J. glanced at the clock on the broadcast booth wall. The six o'clock news segment would be over in a few minutes, and she'd be back on the air. She clamped her headphones on and reached over to help Councilman Caleb Lawrence adjust his. When Harley had booked the councilman as a guest, C.J. had been surprised. Caleb had a reputation for being uncooperative with the media. Still upset over finding Mary's body, C.J. hoped she could concentrate enough to do a decent job with the night's show.

This was the first time she'd met Caleb Lawrence. The pictures in the newspaper didn't do him justice. Widely hailed as one of the best tennis players in the city, he probably had his long hours on the courts to thank for his muscular body. A touch of gray in the dark hair above his ears added sophistication to his appearance. Rumor had it that even though he'd been married for twenty-five years, he was still quite the ladies' man.

He winked at C.J. and patted the headphones into position. "Never had a pair of these on before."

"I'd think someone in your position would have done lots of interviews."

He shook his head. "All my radio campaign ads were recorded in the studio so they could be edited." He pulled his chair a little closer to hers. "This is the first time I've agreed to do a live interview. I'm glad it's with such a good-looking reporter. Maybe you can hold my hand through the whole thing."

"Just relax, Mr. Lawrence, and you'll be fine." She pointed to the next room where Harley and Gwen were lining up the calls. "Harley and Gwen will be screening. I'll find out what the question is before I ask you to address it."

He smiled and leaned closer, his hand grazing her knee. "Thanks. What say we grab a bite of dinner after this show's over? I know a quiet little restaurant that serves a great steak."

She stiffened. "I know you're married."

He laughed. "What difference does that make?"

She bit her tongue in disgust at the arrogant man sitting next to her. What a jerk. He didn't even realize how ridiculous he sounded. What his poor wife must have to endure.

She pulled the microphone forward and adjusted her headphones. "We're getting ready to go on the air."

Caleb, seemingly oblivious to her cool tone, removed some papers from a notebook and laid them on the console in front of him.

In the next room Harley counted down. He pointed to her, and she pulled the microphone closer. "And so I'm back and happy to welcome City Councilman Caleb Lawrence to *C.J.'s Journal* for the next hour. Thanks for dropping by to chat with me, Councilman Lawrence."

Caleb leaned forward. "Thanks for having me, C.J." His cocky, flirtatious tone of a few minutes before was gone, replaced by a businesslike demeanor.

C.J. breathed an inward sigh of relief. The way Caleb had come on to her she thought the broadcast was going to be a disaster, but maybe she was wrong. "I understand you're about to complete your second term in office."

"That's correct."

"And you're getting ready to campaign for a third term?"

Caleb nodded to her. "Yes, I am. I've enjoyed representing the citizens of Oxford, and I look forward to continuing my service."

"Well, I'm sure our listeners have lots of questions to ask you. Let's get right to it and take your first call. Hello, caller. Welcome. What's on your mind tonight?"

"My name is Donna, and I'm the wife of a policeman," the woman said. "My husband puts his life on the line every day on the streets of this city. But our officers can't keep up with the increased drug traffic and the rising crime rate. They need more manpower. When is the city going to address this problem and hire some new officers?"

"Good question, Donna." She glanced at Caleb. "How do you respond to her?"

Caleb loosened his tie and smiled. "We have one of the best-trained police forces in the state. Our officers have gained recognition for their heroism and devotion to duty. The citizens of Oxford don't have to worry. Our police have the crime situation under control."

C.J. remembered conversations she'd heard Mitch have with fellow officers, as well as the city's firefighters, about their concern over budget cuts and lack of equipment. Their frustration with the freeze on hiring had caused many shifts in both departments to work shorthanded.

No wonder crime was rising in the city. The police force was stretched to the limit, and Caleb Lawrence, chairman of the Public Safety Commission, was to blame for a lot of their problems. His refusal to adequately fund the city police and fire departments had placed citizens in danger many times.

She crossed her arms on top of the console and leaned closer to the mic. "Councilman Lawrence is right in his praise of our police department. We should be very proud of every man and woman on the force. They work hard in a dangerous job and often make tremendous sacrifices in their personal lives."

Caleb nodded. "That's right."

She smiled as she glanced at him. "But I think our caller has a concern that needs to be addressed. During the time you've been on the council you've become chairman of the Public Safety Commission. Could you tell our listeners what responsibilities this group has?"

Caleb cleared his throat and took a look at the papers in front of him. "Well, we have several. We appoint the police and fire chiefs, recommend appropriations for the departments to the full council and approve promotions. I suppose you could say we oversee the management and supervision of both departments."

C.J. nodded. "I see. And in the past four years, how many new police officers and firemen would you say have been added to the force?"

Caleb's face flushed. Beads of perspiration dotted his forehead. He shuffled through the papers in front of him. "I don't think I have the numbers on that."

C.J. had never thought of herself as a hard-core news reporter like those she saw on television, but suddenly she wanted the citizens of her town to know how this man had sabotaged their safety.

"Well, let's just take the population increase," she said. "Two years ago the council annexed all the property up to the Cumberland River Bridge. That added about three thousand households to the city. How many police officers and firefighters were hired after that?"

His hands shook, rattling the papers he held. "I'm not sure, but we're always on the lookout for new recruits. I believe Oxford deserves the very best, and I won't hire someone just for the sake of numbers. I want our fine officers to have people they can trust at their sides, those who will strive to give the best protection possible to the citizens of our city."

The man was pathetic. His reply sounded like something a publicist would have written. How had the citizens of Oxford ever elected him? Then she remembered how he'd tried to charm her before the program and how he said he never did live interviews, only recorded ones that could be edited.

C.J. leaned back in her chair. "Thank you, Mr. Lawrence. Let's take another caller."

For the next forty-five minutes, callers attacked Caleb over issues from dissatisfaction with the winner in the Miss Oxford beauty pageant to the price of gasoline. Perspiration poured from his body with each new caller.

C.J. almost felt sorry for him. He'd discarded his crumpled tie and loosened the top buttons on his shirt. His face was bright red. There was no denying it. Caleb Lawrence looked as if he'd been tied up, strapped to a spit and grilled until well-done.

Caleb finished his remarks to a caller, and she noted that the hour was almost up. Time for one more call. She leaned forward. "Hello, caller. Do you have a question for Councilman Lawrence?"

A soft chuckle sounded on the line. "For both of you, C.J."

Her eyes widened. Fala. She should have checked the screen before she answered. Too late she saw the private number displayed. She glanced into the next room where Harley stood alone, grinning at her. He'd pushed his glasses up on his head and stood with his hands on his hips, his sagging pants held up by the belt underneath his potbelly.

She swallowed. "What's your question?"

"I was just thinking about poor Mary Warren and wondered if the councilman knows whether the police have any leads in her murder yet."

Caleb pulled the microphone toward him. "Not yet, but we expect to apprehend this lunatic soon."

C.J. shook her head and grabbed for the mic, but he pushed her hand away.

"Lunatic?" The voice on the line drawled. "Do you really think that's what the killer is?"

"Don't answer that," she whispered, but Caleb ignored her.

Caleb laughed and leaned forward. "Well, of course he is. He's got to be a real sicko. No sane person would kill someone like that."

"Oh, you have my attention," Fala gushed. "Like what? Did you see the body?"

Caleb frowned and hesitated for a moment. "Well, no. But any murder is gruesome."

A long sigh reverberated over the phone. "You don't know how beautiful it really was. Want me to tell you about it?" Fala's sudden shrill laugh sent shivers up C.J.'s spine and made the hair on her arms stand up.

Caleb's eyebrows shot up, and he turned to face C.J. He leaned over and whispered in her ear. "What's with this guy?"

She pulled the microphone back. "We're not going to discuss this crime on the air. Mary Warren was a wonderful person."

"Sure she was. Right up until her last breath." Fala laughed again. "It's your fault, C.J. You didn't solve the riddle."

C.J. reached for the switch to disconnect the call. "We're through talking."

"Wait! There's one more thing before I go," Fala called out. "Tell your guest he might do a better job as a city councilman if he'd spend less time with his friends like Jimmy Carpenter. Maybe he has a reason for not wanting to hire more policemen."

Caleb Lawrence bolted up from his seat. "You're a liar!"

Fala laughed. "We'll see. And C.J., don't forget to check your e-mail."

The line went dead, and C.J. looked at the clock. Thirty seconds left for her program. She reached over and switched her microphone off. If Harley didn't want dead air, let him fill it.

Without a word to Caleb she jerked her headphones off and rushed from the room. She ran to her office and fell into her chair behind the computer. Within moments her e-mails came into view.

Fala had meant it. Another message had arrived. She opened it and read as the message appeared.

Three there are that still stand tall.
One will take a mighty fall.
Another day, or maybe more,
Someone else steps through death's door.
Fala

C.J. stared at the computer screen, unable to move. The words made no more sense to her than the first messages had. *Mitch,* she thought. *I need to call him.* She reached for the phone, but loud voices in the hallway outside her office caught her attention. Caleb Lawrence was yelling at Harley.

A twinge of guilt pricked her at how hard she'd pushed Caleb to address many of the callers' questions. She shook her head and stood up. There was something about Caleb Lawrence she didn't trust, and it wasn't the fact that he was a womanizer.

The image he wanted his constituents to see was of a trusted public official with Oxford's best interests at heart, but Fala had hinted at something else. Perhaps as a journalist, she should take a closer look at his record.

She rose from her chair and stepped into the hall. Caleb Lawrence, his index finger jabbing her producer in the chest, stood in front of Harley.

"You set me up!" Caleb Lawrence yelled at Harley for the

third time. "And that so-called talk show host of yours made me look like a fool."

Where was Gwen? She usually was the voice of reason.

C.J.'s head pounded, and she rubbed her temples to relieve the pressure. "Mr. Lawrence, if you'll just calm down…"

He whirled to face her and shook his finger. "Calm down? How dare you say that! You invite me on your program to talk about my reelection campaign, flirt with me, and then end up ridiculing me before every listener in the city."

C.J. came closer, her voice shaking with rage. "I can't help it if you chose to be less than truthful with your constituents."

Red splotches covered Caleb's face, and a speck of white spittle lined the corner of his mouth. "You're going to be sorry for that remark. I'm going to lodge a complaint against you with your station manager."

C.J. met his stare without flinching. "Your threats don't scare me."

Caleb sucked in his breath and glared at her. "Maybe mine don't, but that last caller seemed to know an awful lot about you. If that really was Mary Warren's killer, I'd say you have a lot more than me to worry about."

Fear stabbed at her, but she forced a smile to her lips and arched an eyebrow. "He seemed to know a lot about you, too." She took a step forward. "Just how well do you know Jimmy Carpenter?"

Caleb studied her for a moment. "You'd better watch it, missy. You're making some powerful enemies in Oxford. Maybe you'd like to borrow this."

His hand flashed from his pocket, his fingers opening to reveal the pearl handle of a knife. It glinted in the light from the overhead fixture. "This is what I carry for protection."

C.J. stepped backward. "Put that thing away."

Caleb Lawrence laughed and dropped the knife back in his

pocket. "Don't like my little toy, huh? Well, neither will any-body who deals with me. That includes your caller and Jimmy Carpenter."

Harley stepped in front of C.J. "I think you're blaming us for something that wasn't our fault. You were asked legitimate questions. It's your problem if members of the audience didn't like the answers."

C.J. felt a hand on her arm and turned to see Gwen. "What's going on?"

She grabbed Gwen's hand and pulled her several feet down the hall. "Where have you been?" she hissed.

Gwen looked at Caleb, her eyes wide, and then back to C.J. "In my office. I had to get away from Harley." She edged closer to C.J. "What's wrong with Mr. Lawrence?"

"He's angry about the program and he's threatening all sorts of things."

The front door on the first floor slammed, and footsteps pounded on the stairs. C.J. and Gwen stepped to the second-floor landing and peered downward. Michael Grayson, his face red with anger, bounded up the stairs and stopped in front of them.

"Well, C.J., you've really done it this time," Michael snarled.

C.J. frowned and stared at him. "What?"

He clenched his teeth and nodded toward Caleb Lawrence several feet away. "I heard your broadcast. You've just made one of our biggest advertisers look like a complete idiot. We'll be lucky if he doesn't pull every penny out of here."

She stepped back against the wall and wrapped her arms around her waist. "I didn't think about that."

"Well, you should have."

C.J. reached out toward him. "Michael, I'm sorry if I've caused you any problems."

Michael regarded her with a cool expression. "It's not just

me, C.J. It's everybody who expects a paycheck from this place." He straightened his shoulders. "Now let me see if I can calm Caleb down."

"Caleb, I'm so sorry," Michael said, walking toward him and Harley. Both men turned to face him.

Caleb held up a hand to quiet him. "Don't say anything, Michael. As far as I'm concerned, this station is no longer advertising for my car dealership. My ads are off the air immediately. Maybe the people at the *Sentinel* will appreciate my support more than your staff seems to."

Caleb stormed away, Michael right behind. "Please, can't we work this out?" Michael called.

"No!" Caleb glared at C.J. a few moments before he turned and stomped down the stairs. Harley ambled over and stopped next to C.J. and Gwen as the downstairs door slammed.

"Well, girls, I'd say we had quite a night. Even if Caleb's angry, you handled him like a pro, C.J. And Fala's call ought to kick our ratings over the top."

Michael grabbed Harley by the shirt and shoved him against the wall, his nose just inches from Harley's. "Now you listen to me, you little pipsqueak. You humiliated a city councilman and catered to a confessed murderer. Your poor judgment has caused us more trouble than I even want to think about right now. I'm the one who'll have to tell the station manager about this. I suggest that if you want to save your job, you find Caleb, and make this right—no matter what you have to do. Understand?"

Harley swallowed. He reached up under Michael's arms and knocked his hands off him. "Okay, Michael. No need to get upset. I'll take care of it."

Michael pulled the cuffs of his jacket over his wrists, straightened his shoulders and stared at Harley. "See that you do."

He turned and walked down the steps, leaving the three of

them standing in silence until he'd gone. Then Harley spoke. "Now don't you two worry."

Tears puddled in Gwen's eyes. "What if we all get fired?"

Harley's eyes softened, his gaze on Gwen. "I'm not going to let anything happen to you. Caleb eats at a downtown restaurant most nights. Maybe if I'm lucky I can catch him there." He headed down the stairs, but stopped and turned back. "I hate to leave you alone in the building, especially with Fala around. Do you want to leave with me?"

C.J. shook her head. "I've got a few things to do before I go home."

Harley glanced at Gwen. "What about you? Want me to walk you to your car?"

Gwen stepped closer to C.J. "No, thanks. I'll wait for C.J."

Harley smiled at her. "Have a nice weekend. I'll see you on Monday. I'll close up. When you leave, the front door will lock behind you." He turned and disappeared down the steps.

C.J. watched him go and then headed back to her office. Thirty minutes later as she studied Fala's message looking for a clue, the door opened and Gwen walked in, her coat draped over her arm.

"It's starting to snow, and I don't like to drive when the streets are slick. Are you ready to go?"

"Snow?" C.J. rose, opened the blinds, and peered out the window. Already a layer of white dusted the ledge. "I won't stay much longer, either, but you've already worked way past your time today. Go home, and I'll call you tomorrow."

"Thanks." Gwen waved and disappeared down the hall.

C.J. turned her attention back to the computer screen. She reread the message, repeating it until she could recite every word. There had to be a clue in it about who would be murdered.

Think, her mind screamed. Solve the riddle before someone else dies.

A tap at the window sent her bolting to her feet. She whirled around, her hands holding on to the desk behind her, and peered through the blinds into the night.

A terrible fear washed over her. Fala knew too much about her life and habits. Maybe he was outside the radio station just waiting to make her his next victim.

SIX

The snow drifted through the bare branches and formed an outline around Fala's boots as it fell silently on the hardened earth. Staring at the radio station across the street, Fala remained motionless between the trees.

One after another they'd left. All except C.J. Her office light was still on. Perhaps she'd read the e-mail by now. But she hadn't solved it. And she never would. Not until it was too late. That's the way it always was.

The wind whistled through the branches, and Fala pulled his coat tighter. In the station's parking lot swirls of white blew across the pavement. Soon the asphalt would shine like a blanket of diamonds in the lights that illuminated the marked spaces.

White. Just like Mary's bedroom. Fala flipped the cigarette butt toward the ground, reached into the coat pocket and drew out a handkerchief. Crimson stains stood out against the milky background.

Fala raised the handkerchief and nuzzled it. "Mary, you'll be with me forever."

The light in C.J.'s office still burned. Foolish girl. Her tirade on the program had been comical. Did she really think she could stop what was about to happen?

With eyes shut, Fala inhaled. *I'm close, C.J. Can you feel me?*

Time for the next move. Blood flowing onto white snow. What could be more beautiful?

Terror engulfed C.J. as the tapping at the window grew louder. The wind whistled around the corner of the building. Then she saw it. A tree limb rapped on the glass.

She pressed her hand to her chest and bent over in relief. Nothing out there. Fala would have to be part spider to scale the side of the brick building to reach her second-floor office.

She straightened and stared at the tree limb, still visible in the darkness. Some deep need to know for sure urged her toward the window. *I'm being paranoid,* she thought. She hesitated. What would she do if something—or someone— peered back?

She reached for the cord of the blinds, but hesitated before pulling it. Backing away, she crossed the room and turned off the light. Returning to the window, she peered through the open slats.

Her gaze traveled over the deserted lot, the street beyond, and lingered on the woods directly across from the station. Something about the bare trees held her attention. Last summer she and Gwen had walked down the path that wound through the lush growth to the next street. Wildflowers grew in abundance there, making it look like an enchanted forest.

The snow stopped for just a moment, giving her a better view of the trees. What was that she saw? A small flicker of light? At that moment a glow arced through the trees toward the ground.

She searched her memory. Where had she seen something like that before? Her breath caught in her throat, and she closed her eyes at the scene unfolding in her mind. She was a child again, sitting in a car next to a deserted farmhouse where her parents had gone to buy drugs. They stood on the dark porch talking to a man she couldn't see. She watched the small circle glow near the man's face. A cigarette. Suddenly, the cigarette's red tip lit the darkness as it sailed from the porch.

Her eyes flew open, and she stumbled backward. Her foot struck the edge of the desk. Her hand clutched the chair to steady herself. Someone was out there. Fala?

She had to get out of the building. Whirling around, she grabbed her coat and purse and ran from the office down the stairs. At the front door she hesitated before she stepped outside and dashed toward her car.

Snow covered the windshield and the rear glass. *Get in the car,* her mind screamed. No time to clean the windshield. She jumped in and plunged the key into the ignition. The small canister of Mace hooked to her key ring bumped against the steering column. As nervous as she was tonight, she doubted that she could use it in a dangerous situation.

No time to think about that now. She started the motor and turned the windshield wipers on high and adjusted the defroster to full blast. Rolling the window down, she stuck her head out and roared from her parking spot toward the exit.

The thundering rumble of a motorcycle split the night air. It sped past her, its tires throwing snow across her windshield, and skidded to a stop across the entrance to the parking lot.

She screamed and jammed the brakes to the floorboard. A grinding screech filled the air as the car slid to the right on the slippery asphalt. She wrenched the wheel to the left and shrieked in fear. The car jumped the curb, plowed across the parking lot and came to rest near a light pole.

The motorcycle engine revved, and the bike pulled forward. It came to a stop in front of her car. The windshield wipers provided a hazy view through the snowy glass as they swished back and forth. A man wearing a long trench coat and a ski cap stared at her. A blond woman bundled in a heavy down jacket and jeans hung on the back. The man's gloved fingers flexed on the handlebars. Without looking down, he switched off the motor, hit the kickstand and climbed off, the blonde right behind him.

He stood with his legs slightly spread. A sinister smile curled his lips. The overhead streetlight cast an eerie glow across his face and highlighted a jagged scar from the side of his nose to his left ear. He glared at her for a moment and then stomped toward her. The snow crunched under his heavy boots.

Though she'd never seen him in person, she knew who he was right away—Jimmy Carpenter. Her numbed fingers fumbled to put the car in Reverse, but the gearshift slipped from her grasp.

He stopped beside her window and laughed. "Where do you think you're going, Miss C.J. Tanner?" His hand snaked through the window and switched off the ignition.

"Wh-what do you want?"

"To talk to you," he snarled. "Git out."

The woman, her hand on her hip, stood next to Jimmy. "She don't look so tough now, does she, Jimmy?"

"Naw." He leaned over, his arms resting on the bottom opening of the window. "More like a scared rabbit, I'd say." He stared at her for a moment. "I said git out."

She shook her head. "No, leave me alone."

With a growl he jerked the door open, grabbed her arm, and pulled her out of the car. His fingers cut into her arm as he dragged her toward him and slammed the door. With a shove he released her, and she fell back against the car.

Her first impulse was to try to push past the two and run screaming into the night. Perhaps a passerby would help her. Her gaze darted toward the deserted street. The snow must have kept most people home. She forced herself to relax and straightened to her full height. She fought to control the trembling of her voice and raised an eyebrow.

"W-well, if i-it isn't J-Jimmy C-Carpenter, resident drug dealer and a threat to every ch-child in Oxford."

He gritted his teeth and drew back his hand. "You've got a smart mouth, lady. Maybe I need to shut it for you."

"Yeah, Jimmy, teach her a lesson," the woman jeered. Her blond curls bounced around the band of the earmuffs clamped on her head.

C.J. turned to stare at the woman. "Brought your own cheering section, huh?"

The blonde glared at her. "Don't let her talk to me that way, Jimmy. Show her you mean business."

"Shut up, Didi," Jimmy growled. "Let me handle this."

C.J. clenched her fists at her side to conceal how much her hands shook. "Does it make you feel like a big man to threaten a woman?" She glanced at Didi. "Your girlfriend may be used to it, but it doesn't work with me. I suggest you get on your bike and leave before I press charges against you."

Jimmy pulled the glove off his right hand and shook his balled fist in her face. "Let me suggest something to you. Stop making me the subject of your show, or you're gonna be real sorry."

A tattooed skull and crossbones covered the top of his hand. She turned her head slightly and felt her stomach heave. She forced a frown to her face and leaned forward. "The police are onto you, Mr. Drug Lord. Your days are numbered in Oxford, and if I can do anything to speed that up, I'll be glad to help."

He lowered his fist and licked his lips. "Quite a little spit-fire, ain't ya? When I get through with you, you'll be sorry you ever messed with Jimmy Carpenter."

She tilted her head to one side and studied Jimmy. He'd had a chance to hurt her ever since he'd ridden up, but so far he'd only tried to scare her. Why was that? She stared into his eyes, searching for an answer.

He blinked from her intense scrutiny and turned away. In that brief moment she sensed the truth. He hadn't come here to hurt her. He was only trying to intimidate her. The thought sent relief surging through her.

She stepped forward, her foot pressing on his boot. "Move. You're blocking my way."

He gave her one more menacing look before he headed toward the motorcycle. "Get on, Didi."

Didi ran after him. "You ain't gonna leave it like that, are you?"

The woman cowered as he grabbed her arm with one hand and raised the other. "I said get on," he yelled.

C.J. stood with the snow swirling around her and watched the bike disappear in the distance. When it was out of sight, she yanked the car door open and jumped in. The key ring jingled against the steering column before the motor roared to life. Cold air gushed from the defroster.

She twisted in her seat and pushed at the buttons on the door's side panel. The windows rose, and the locks clicked. Every nerve ending in her body screamed. She wrapped her arms around the steering wheel to calm down.

Through the windshield she could now see the woods across the street and remembered the light arcing through the darkness. Had someone been watching from there? Fala? Or Jimmy? She shivered. Or maybe they were one and the same.

She pressed the accelerator and headed toward the exit. The headlights illuminated the motorcycle's path in the snow. She glanced from the tracks to the woods. Tonight had confirmed her worst fear—evil had invaded her world.

It had been a long day. Mitch was tired and needed to go home, but something kept him at the office even after all his reports were done. Maybe it was the memory of Mary's bedroom, or perhaps it was the fear he'd seen in C.J.'s eyes when she'd handed him the e-mails.

Fala. Mitch leaned back in his desk chair, tented his fingers and tapped them together. He'd never heard that name before. Maybe there was something he was overlooking. Could the killer be leaving a clue with the name he'd chosen to use?

Mitch reached toward the computer keyboard and typed the word *Fala* into the search engine he used. Within seconds the screen flooded with sites—all of them related to Franklin Roosevelt's Scottish terrier. That hardly seemed logical. Why would a killer use the name of a famous presidential pet?

Another thought struck Mitch, and he typed *The name Fala* into the search engine. The first result brought a smile to his face—What does the name Fala mean?

He clicked the link and read aloud. "A Native American male name. The meaning—a crow."

For a few seconds Mitch pondered the words on the screen. "A crow?" he murmured. Could there be some special significance to the name?

On impulse he typed *crow* in and began to click through the search results. The information he read about the habits of crows raised some new questions in his mind. He reached for a pen to make some notes just as the phone rang.

"Hello."

"Mitch, this is Cara Evans."

He smiled at the husky voice of the assistant district attorney. She and C.J. had been friends ever since they met at the dinner when the police department honored him with a Meritorious Service Award—the department's highest honor. "Hi, Cara. How are you tonight?"

She sighed. "Still at the office, as you are. I wanted to catch you before you left."

He sat down at his desk. "What can I do for you?"

"Did you hear C.J.'s show?"

His fingers tightened around a pencil that lay in front of him. "No. Did you?"

"Yeah. Fala called in again."

The pencil snapped in half. "And?"

"Fala might as well have admitted to killing Mary Warren. And C.J. was told to check her e-mail."

His fist pounded the desk. "I warned her to be careful. I can't understand why Harley would even put that call through to her."

"Neither can I." Cara paused a moment. "Mitch, I'm worried about C.J. She's getting in way over her head with this character. I'm afraid she's in danger."

"I am, too. I've just been searching the Internet and found out some very interesting information."

"Tell me," she said.

Mitch took a deep breath. "I don't know if this means anything or not, but it made me rethink my first impression of the murderer. I found out that the name *Fala* means crow."

"You mean, like the bird?"

"Yeah, but that's not the part that caught my attention. I didn't know that a group of crows is called a murder. They're named that because they often kill crows that don't belong in their territory. Then they feed on the dead birds' carcasses."

A gasp sounded on the line. "Oh, Mitch, what could this mean?"

Mitch raked his hand through his hair and shook his head. "I don't know. I've been trying to figure it out. It could just be a coincidence that he chose that name, but that seems unlikely. Or it could mean that Fala is more than one person—a group—and they're trying to get rid of somebody who doesn't belong, or somebody who threatens them."

"Like Jimmy Carpenter and his drug ring?"

Mitch exhaled. "Exactly."

"Then you've got to warn C.J."

"She won't listen to me anymore. In fact, she acts like she hates me."

Cara's throaty chuckle vibrated in his ear. "Don't be put off by what she says. I know how much she loved you, and you don't just stop having those feelings overnight."

Mitch took a deep breath. "So what should I do?"

"Go to her. Explain how dangerous this is getting. I think she needs protection."

Mitch stood up. Even though he'd vowed earlier today that he would stay away from her, he didn't want to see her get hurt. "You're right. I'll go by her house on my way home."

"You do that. I'll talk to you tomorrow."

"Goodnight, Cara."

He started to hang up the phone, but Cara's voice called out. "Mitch."

He put the receiver back to his ear. "Yes?"

"You will catch Fala."

"I hope so."

He placed the handset in the cradle and grabbed his jacket. As he approached his office door, it opened and Myra walked in.

"Glad I caught you before you left."

He shrugged his arms into the coat sleeves and adjusted the collar. "What can I do for you, Myra?"

She smiled. "I thought we might get a bite to eat before we go home. Want to join me for a little Chinese food?"

"Sorry. I'm on my way over to C.J.'s. Let me take a rain check on that."

"Sure, Mitch. Go on. I'll see you in the morning."

Pulling his car keys from his pocket, he hurried down the hall. Cara's words about how much C.J. had loved him sent a warm rush through him. In the same instant, cruel reality struck him. Cara also thought C.J. might be at risk. If that was the case, there was no time to waste. Fala was becoming more dangerous by the moment, and Mitch had to do whatever was needed to protect the woman he loved.

SEVEN

C.J. sat at her kitchen table, her fingers wrapped around a coffee mug. She raised the cup to her mouth and sipped. The hot liquid scalded her throat, but she didn't flinch. Her body shook from the cold—not just the chill of the weather, but the iciness of fear that still flowed through her veins.

She couldn't believe how she'd talked to Jimmy. And on top of that, she'd practically challenged Fala on her program. She set the mug on the table and rubbed her forehead.

The doorbell rang, sending the chimes of Big Ben echoing through the house. She pushed up from the table and eased through the dark hall into the living room. The porch light shone through the small oval glass at the top of the front door. She ducked into the living room and pulled the curtain of the window back to get a glimpse of who was there.

Mitch stood at the door, his shoulders hunched forward in the cold. Tears filled her eyes, and she pressed her hand against her pounding heart. She'd never been so glad to see anybody in her life.

She jerked the door open. "Mitch, come in. What are you doing out on a night like this?"

He stomped the snow from his feet, stepped into the house and closed the door behind him. "I've thought about you all day, and I wanted to check on you before I went back to my apartment."

His eyes held a worried look as his gaze searched her face. The dam within her cracked, and tears gushed from her eyes. "Oh, Mitch," she cried, "I'm so scared."

She didn't know who made the first move, but suddenly she was in his arms with her cheek resting against his chest. For the first time since this nightmare began, she felt safe. The leather jacket he wore smelled of his aftershave. She closed her eyes and inhaled the aroma for added strength.

He nuzzled at her ear, his husky voice soothing her. "Shhh. It's all right. I'm here."

C.J.'s eyes opened. After a moment, she drew back and wiped away her tears. The sheen of moisture blurred her vision. They stood facing each other, the connection broken.

"I'm sorry. I didn't mean to fall to pieces on you. I guess everything's catching up to me."

"You've had a rough day." His shoulders slumped as he released his hold on her.

Looking toward the kitchen, she said, "Would you like a cup of coffee?"

"Sure."

He followed her into the kitchen and stopped next to the counter where the coffeepot sat. They reached for a cup on the shelf at the same time, their fingers colliding in midair. She jerked away at the searing contact.

"Sorry," he said and pulled a mug from the shelf.

She nodded, backed away and fell down in the chair where she'd sat earlier. The five o'clock shadow on his face intensified his rugged good looks and set her heart to pounding. She glanced away as he turned and sat down across from her.

They sipped in silence for a moment before he cleared his throat. "I had a call from Cara before I left the office."

"Oh?"

"She said Fala called you again tonight. She's concerned about you."

C.J. nodded. "I have to admit I'm a little spooked myself."

He frowned and leaned forward. "What happened?"

For the next few minutes he listened as she told him about her broadcast and the events afterward. For some reason she stopped before telling him about the encounter with Jimmy Carpenter. Mitch had warned her about putting suspected lawbreakers in the spotlight, and she had charged ahead as usual without following his advice.

"After I read the e-mail, I left as fast as I could and drove home." She took a sip from her cup. "I guess I still hadn't recovered when you arrived."

He folded his arms on the table and stared at her. "It's understandable. Mary was our friend. What we saw in her house today was enough to haunt even the toughest police officer."

"It was horrible."

He nodded. "I know how upset you are." He swallowed before he spoke. "C.J., I don't want it to be awkward because I'm here. Especially with our history. But you have to remember that I'm a policeman, and I have a job to do."

His words stung her. Their history? Was that what she had become to him? She should be happy he'd finally accepted her decision to call off the wedding, but deep in her heart she knew she wasn't. Her lips trembled. "I'm glad you came." The hall clock chimed at that moment, and she gasped. "It's eight-thirty. Have you had supper?"

He shook his head. "I came straight here from the office."

"I have some steaks I can broil in no time. Want to eat dinner with me?"

A smile spread across his face. "That sounds great. I'm getting a little hungry."

She jumped up and hurried to the refrigerator. Pulling the package of meat out, she turned to find him right behind her. She held the steaks between them like a shield. "I didn't hear you."

He stepped aside and reached around her into the refrigerator. "Why don't I make a salad while you put the steaks up?"

Her fingers trembled as she set the wrapped package on the counter and washed her hands. Behind her the refrigerator door closed, and Mitch whistled a little tune as he placed the vegetables on the cutting board.

He stuck his hands underneath the faucet and scrubbed as he hummed. Pulling a paper towel from the roll, he leaned against the counter and smiled. This was too familiar. The past was replaying itself in front of her. It seemed like old times, but she knew it wasn't.

It would be so easy to go to him, wrap her arms around his waist and lay her cheek on his chest. She longed for the times when she had done that, but they were gone. She'd given it up for a career that was now threatening to challenge her sanity, and she had no one to blame but herself.

Mitch swallowed the last bite on his plate and laid his knife and fork aside. It had been a long time since he'd enjoyed a meal so much. And it wasn't just the food. It was being with C.J. again. He'd never dreamed when he dropped by to check on her that they would end up having dinner together, but here they were sitting across from each other.

Even though she'd been quiet through a lot of the meal, she'd joined in the conversation enough to let him know she was glad he was there. Or was that just wishful thinking on his part?

She'd even bowed her head when he said grace before they ate, something she hadn't done in the past. He dared let himself hope she might be opening herself up to God's presence in her life.

He put his napkin beside his plate. "That was delicious. I don't know when I've eaten so well."

Her eyes studied his face. "Are you eating all right? I think you've lost weight."

He grinned and patted his stomach. "You can't get rid of extra pounds when you live on pizza and hamburgers."

She pushed her plate aside and pulled her coffee cup toward her. "I have pound cake I bought at the bakery. How about a piece with a cup of coffee? We can take it in the den."

He stood up and began to clear the table. "Let me help you with these."

Her hand on his arm stopped him. "I'll just put them in the sink. Go on in the den, and I'll bring the dessert."

Pound cake instead of the chocolate she liked? He smiled. She'd bought his favorite dessert.

"Here we are."

He whirled and sucked in his breath at the sight of her coming through the doorway to the den. Steam rose from two cups of coffee. Slabs of cake sat on her best china. In the lamplight's glow, she'd never looked more beautiful.

She set the tray on the coffee table and took a seat on the couch. He dropped down beside her and reached for the cake. His shaking fingers fumbled to grasp a fork. She didn't seem to notice as she picked up a coffee cup.

Scooting back into the cushions of the couch, she drew her feet up under her. "I'm glad you came by tonight. The house was way too quiet."

He nodded, the cake sticking in his throat. Grabbing the coffee, he swallowed and glanced over at her. Although he'd wanted to see her, he still had a job to do. He started to tell her what he'd discovered about Fala's name, but decided against it. There was no need to give her something else to worry about. Instead, he said, "Tell me again what Fala's e-mail said."

She frowned and sat up straight, her feet on the floor. "Just that someone else was going to step through death's door. Would you like to read it?"

"Yeah, I would."

C.J. put her dishes back on the tray and walked to the computer. He pulled a chair beside her and sat waiting for it to boot. She pulled the message up and read it aloud.

His forehead wrinkled as he leaned over and reread it. "Does this make sense to you?"

She shook her head. "No. I've racked my brain, but I can't figure it out. Do you see anything I've overlooked?"

"Another day," he murmured. "That may mean we have some time before he strikes again. Maybe the lab can come up with something from Mary's murder."

She sat back in her chair and crossed her arms. "I hope so. But why is Fala sending me these e-mails?"

He shook his head. "I don't know."

A soft chime from the computer announced the arrival of a new message. She stared at him, her eyes wide. She clicked the in-box and gasped. "Mitch, it's from Fala."

He edged closer. "What does it say?"

Their heads almost touched as they leaned toward the screen. She took a deep breath and clicked the mouse. Fala's latest missive came into view.

Another gone, oh hear him cry,
Asking why you made him die.
You chose the one, now you know
When he agreed to do your show.
Fala

The chair tumbled backward as C.J. sprang up. Mitch, from his seat next to her, grabbed for it and righted it. He turned back to the e-mail and read it once more before he looked up at her.

"Can you remember everyone you've had on your show?" he asked.

"Don't you see, Mitch?" she screamed. "He's talking about Caleb Lawrence."

Mitch stood and grabbed her by the shoulders. "We can't be sure. You've interviewed lots of people since you went on the air."

Her body shook. "But Fala called in tonight and insinuated that Caleb was a friend of Jimmy Carpenter's. Caleb was so angry."

"With good reason. A city councilman doesn't need to be tied to a suspected crook."

She nodded and sat back down in the chair. She stared at the screen for a moment before she looked up. "But it was more that that. There was something threatening in Fala's voice. Caleb was so upset that he showed us a knife he carried for protection."

Mitch sat down beside her. "What kind of knife?"

"It had a pearl handle. It looked like an antique switchblade."

Mitch pulled his cell phone from his pocket and speed-dialed the department. "I'd better call the station and tell them to get some officers over to Caleb's house. He needs to be warned."

"Oxford Police."

"Chet, this is Mitch Harmon. I…"

"Mitch," the night dispatcher interrupted, "I was just getting ready to call you. We've just gotten a call that Caleb Lawrence's body was found in an alley behind Justine's Restaurant. The chief wants you down there right away."

Mitch swallowed. "I'm on my way." He flipped the cell phone closed.

"What is it?" The words seemed to catch in her throat.

"We were too late. Caleb Lawrence's body was just discovered in a downtown alley."

A gasp escaped from her mouth as she clamped her hand over it. Her head shook back and forth. "Why is Fala doing this?"

He put his arm around her shoulders and drew her closer to him. "Even though it seems likely at this point, we can't be sure the two deaths are connected. I'll know more when I get down there." He tightened his hold. "But I don't want to leave you here alone."

She straightened in the chair. "I'll be all right. You have to do your job. Just let me know what you find out. Okay?"

He stared at her for a moment. "I will. In fact, I'll come back by here."

She followed him as he headed toward the front of the house. At the door her fingers wrapped around his wrist, sending shock waves up his arm. "Be careful, Mitch."

An urge to kiss her welled up in him. He swallowed and licked his lips. "I will. Don't open the door for anyone but me."

Before he could give in to his impulse, he turned and ran for his car.

EIGHT

The flashing lights on the squad cars blinked patterns of blue across the brick buildings lining the alley. The area bustled with activity as it had ever since Mitch's arrival a few minutes earlier. Mitch and Myra stood by the Dumpster behind Justine's Restaurant and silently surveyed the crime scene. Caleb Lawrence's body, now covered with a blanket, lay sprawled in the middle of the narrow street.

Sergeant Matthew Borden, the first officer to respond, stopped beside them. "One of the kitchen employees came outside to empty some trash and found him. He said there was so much blood he didn't get close. Just ran back in and called 9-1-1."

A gust of wind stirred the snow at Mitch's feet as it blew across the pavement. "Does it appear as if robbery might be the motive?"

The officer shook his head. "He had several thousand dollars in his wallet."

Myra frowned at Mitch. "That's a lot of money to be carrying around."

Mitch nodded. "Yeah. Evidently the killer wasn't interested in it." Then he asked Sergeant Borden, "What else did you find?"

"Some keys and a handkerchief were in his pants pocket. There was a small appointment book in his coat."

"How about a pearl-handled knife?"

The sergeant shook his head. "No sign of one. Why?"

"He had one earlier tonight when he left WLMT. Are you sure it's not beside the body?"

"We searched the area. Any footprints around the body had been brushed away, but we did find some over there by the building." The sergeant inclined his head toward the wall close to the corner of the alley.

"How many?"

The officer pulled his hat lower on his head. "Hard to tell. Looks like there may have been a scuffle. We found some boot tracks and some smaller prints. I'd guess they belong to a man and a woman."

Mitch frowned. Two people. Maybe his suspicion about more than one killer might be right. "But those prints weren't near the body?"

Sergeant Borden shook his head. "No, they led away from the alley and across the parking lot, where we lost them." The officer's lapel microphone squawked, and he stepped away from Mitch and Myra. "Excuse me. I need to take this."

Mitch squatted next to Caleb's body, lifted the blanket and stared for a moment before he recovered the corpse and pushed to his feet. "We have two deaths, both victims stabbed to death. One has bloody handprints left everywhere. The other has a knife missing. What's the connection?"

Myra shook her head. "I don't know." She glanced at the backdoor of the restaurant. "Shouldn't we question the employees? They probably want to go home."

"Yeah. Let's do that."

As they turned to enter the restaurant, Jeff Parker, the coroner, rose to his feet from his squatting position next to the body. He walked toward Mitch.

"What've you got, Jeff?" Mitch asked as he approached.

Jeff held up a glass vial for them to see. "A blond hair in his hand. Stab wounds, just like on Mrs. Warren's body. This guy isn't just a killer, he's a butcher."

The wind whistled around them, and Myra shoved her hands deeper in her coat pockets. "How long would you say he's been dead?"

Jeff shrugged. "With the weather conditions, it's hard to tell. Maybe an hour or two."

Mitch nodded. "Let us know if you turn up anything else. We're going to question the employees."

An eerie silence greeted Mitch and Myra as they stepped through the rear entrance into a storage room. An overhead light burned in the area where boxes sat stacked on top of each other along the walls. On the opposite side of the room, a closed door led into the kitchen, and they pushed through it.

The gleaming stainless-steel work areas of the kitchen looked as if they'd been cleaned for the night, and the range and grill were turned off. A thump behind them caused Myra to whirl around in the direction of the sound, her hand on her gun.

Her body relaxed, and she smiled as she caught sight of the ice machine. "Guess I'm a little jumpy."

Mitch laughed and headed to the swinging door that led into the dining room. "We've had enough today to make anyone skittish."

As they stepped into the elegant dining area, Mitch remembered the last time he'd been in this room. He'd brought C.J. here for dinner the night he'd asked her to marry him. During dessert he'd slipped the ring box across the table. When she opened it, her eyes had lit up and they'd promised to love each other forever.

He shook the memory from his mind and turned toward the employees who sat together at a large table near the rear of the room. A woman who appeared to be in her late forties, a scarf tied around her dark hair and her fur coat draped over the back of her chair, sat drinking a cup of coffee. Her brown eyes looked red, as if she'd been crying. She rose to meet them and held out a slender hand, adorned with several diamond rings.

"I'm Justine Blair. One of my employees called and told me what had happened, and I came back to see if I could be of assistance."

Mitch shook her hand. "I'm Detective Harmon, and this is Detective Summers. I know who you are, Mrs. Blair. I've seen you when I've eaten here."

She took a step forward and looked from him to Myra. "I can't tell you how upsetting this is. Mr. Lawrence was a regular customer and a very good friend. Do you have any idea who might have done this?"

Myra shook her head. "No, ma'am. But we'd like to ask your employees a few questions."

She bit her lip, and Mitch could see tears in her eyes. "By all means." She closed her eyes and rubbed her forehead with her fingertips. "Detectives, would you care for some coffee?"

"No, thanks," Myra said as she pulled a small notebook from her pocket. "We'll try to make this as quick as possible."

Justine glanced toward the kitchen. "What about the officers outside? I would go out and ask them, but I don't think I could stand to see poor Caleb." A tear trickled down the side of her face.

"That's not necessary," Mitch said. "But thanks."

Directing his words to Myra, Mitch said, "Why don't you question the guy who found the body, and I'll talk to the waitress and hostess who saw Caleb leave?"

Myra nodded and faced the group, her gaze flitting across the faces of the gathered employees. "Now which one of you discovered the body?"

* * *

Forty-five minutes later, Justine locked the back door of the restaurant as Mitch and Myra stepped back outside. During the time they were inside, things had calmed down and only Sergeant Borden and two other officers remained. Mitch caught a glimpse of the ambulance carrying Caleb Lawrence's body as it disappeared around the corner, bound for the morgue.

He asked Myra, "Did you learn anything?"

She shook her head. "Nobody in the kitchen saw or heard anything until one of the workers came outside to dump some trash. What about you?"

Mitch smiled. "Linda and Samantha had some information. They both saw a man join Caleb, and they argued. Linda heard him call the man Harley."

Myra looked at him, a quizzical look on her face. "I've heard that name somewhere before."

Mitch chuckled. "Probably from me. From the description they gave, it matches C.J.'s producer, Harley Martin."

Myra raised her eyebrows. "Oh."

"But that's not the biggest piece of news. After Harley left, a woman with long, blond hair came in and sat at the table next to Caleb. They'd never seen her before and didn't get her name, but Linda gave me a good description of the cashmere earmuffs she was wearing."

Myra remained lost in thought for a moment. "Jeff said Caleb had a blond hair in his hand."

"Yeah."

Sergeant Borden walked toward them. "I've sent two of my men to inform Caleb's wife. I'll go back to the station and make a report. Are you two going back to the department tonight, or will you file your report in the morning?"

Mitch glanced at Myra. "I told C.J. I'd go back there. Why don't we go to the station and fill out the reports first?"

She nodded. "All right. I'll meet you there."

Mitch followed as Myra walked down the alley toward her car and watched until she'd pulled out into the street. He started to get into his car, but straightened and stared back at the alley. Pulling a flashlight from the glove compartment, he turned back to the spot where Caleb's body had been discovered.

He stood in the middle of the alley, shining the beam from his light along the buildings. Stepping through the snow, he walked the narrow street past Justine's and back. The other officers had searched the scene, but he never liked to leave until he felt satisfied that nothing had been overlooked.

As he passed the Dumpster, the light shone across an area on the ground where the snow was packed harder than in other places. He knelt down and inspected the spot, which seemed to extend to the back of the metal container. The waitress had said Harley left after arguing with Caleb. Could he have stood here waiting for the opportunity to murder Caleb?

Maybe the blonde lured Caleb into the alley where someone—perhaps Harley—waited. The smaller footprints in the snow could have been hers and the larger ones his. If she wasn't involved, where did she go?

From the beginning it had troubled him that Harley had put Fala's calls through to C.J. Maybe he was using the *C.J.'s Journal* as some sort of open forum to publicize Fala's killings. Mitch might not have to look any farther than C.J.'s office for the killer.

Mitch stood up and stared down the alley. Two murders in one day. His stomach roiled at the thought of C.J. at the mercy of this sadistic butcher. No matter how much she protested, he was going to see that she was protected until Fala was caught.

C.J. sat on the couch in her den, her feet pulled up under her and an afghan covering her from head to toe. She hadn't stopped shaking since she received the last e-mail from Fala.

Mitch had promised to come back, but he could be tied up all night. He'd been gone for nearly three hours now, but she couldn't call him. She'd learned a long time ago not to interrupt him when he was conducting an investigation.

She picked up the remote and switched on the television. Late-night talk shows and old movies held no interest for her tonight, and after a few minutes she turned the TV off. Tossing the afghan aside, she rose and headed into the kitchen. Maybe a cup of tea would calm her nerves.

Just as she picked up the teakettle, the doorbell rang. She set the pot on the stove and hurried into the living room to peer out the window. Mitch stood in the glow of the front porch light.

With a cry of relief she ran to the door and jerked it open. "Mitch, thanks for coming back."

He stepped into the hallway, pulled off his gloves and blew on his hands. "It's cold out there. My hands feel like chunks of ice."

She took his arm and drew him toward the kitchen. "I was just going to make some tea. Come have a cup with me."

He followed her and sat at the table while she poured the tea. When she set the cup before him, he took a long sip. "Mmm, that's good."

Her curiosity couldn't be contained any longer. She sank down in the chair across from his and leaned forward. "Tell me what you found."

Between swallows, he told her about the scene in the alley and his questioning of the employees. When he'd finished, a sad look came over his face. His fingers stroked the side of the cup. "You know," he said, "I've seen a lot of death, but there was something about this crime that troubled me. I think it was the feeling I got from talking to the employees that really bothered me."

"What do you mean?"

He crossed his arms on the table and hunched his shoulders. "Well, Justine had been crying and was very upset. But the employees were rather callous about the whole thing."

She tilted her head to one side. "But what was it that bothered you?"

He picked up his cup and stared into it. "As horrible as it was with Mary today, I knew she was a believer and that she was with God. But with Caleb I was left wondering. It made me aware of my responsibility to share my faith with everyone I meet."

The conversation was taking a turn C.J. didn't like, and she searched for something to say. "You said the employees were callous. What did they say?"

"It seemed as if none of them cared for Caleb. In fact, the hostess was really vocal about how he had hit on her earlier."

The memory of Caleb's hand brushing across her knee flashed in her mind. "I can imagine how she felt."

Mitch straightened. "How would you know?"

She felt her face grow warm. "Caleb tried to get me to go to dinner with him after the show."

Mitch's eyes narrowed. "What did you tell him?"

She hesitated. The excuse she'd given Caleb that he was married was reason enough not to go, but C.J. knew that was only a part of it. She couldn't imagine herself ever wanting to be with any man other than Mitch, but that hardly mattered now. She picked up her cup. "That I wasn't interested."

His shoulders relaxed. "That's good."

C.J. drained her cup, stood up and carried it to the sink. Her hands trembled as she set it down. "You said Caleb left with a woman. Do you have any idea who she was?"

Mitch's chair scraped on the floor, and he rose to stand beside her. "No, but we have a description. A blonde wearing expensive earmuffs."

A tremor rippled through her body. She gasped and pulled

a paper towel from the holder. Wiping her hands, she slowly turned and faced him. "Were they cashmere?"

He frowned at her. "How did you know that?"

She tossed the paper towel in the trash can and leaned against the counter. "There's something I didn't tell you about tonight."

"What?"

His eyes grew wide as she related her experience with Jimmy Carpenter and Didi, his girlfriend, earlier in the evening. When she finished, his eyes held an accusing look. "Why didn't you tell me this when I was here before?"

She lifted her chin and crossed her arms. "I didn't think it had anything to do with Fala, and I didn't want to hear you say *I told you so* about my program." C.J. tried to meet his angry gaze, but she wavered and reached for his cup.

"You should have told me. Why do you have to be so independent? Don't you understand that I only care about your safety?"

"If you care about me, then let me make my own decisions, Mitch. Don't try to make me do what you think I should."

Mitch raked his hand through his hair and stood there staring at her for several seconds. "I don't think I'll ever understand you, C.J. I hope someday you can tell me what it is that makes you think I'm out to dominate you. Nothing could be further from the truth."

She wanted to scream at him that she'd heard those same words out of her father's mouth, and they'd been lies. Instead, she turned back to the sink and began to rinse the cups.

Mitch stepped beside her and leaned against the counter. "All right, let's not talk about our problems right now. Let's look at what's happened in the last two days. I think you'd have to agree that this case is getting too complicated. I don't know if there's any connection between Fala and Jimmy Carpenter, but they both seem to have an interest in you. That puts you in a dangerous position."

"There's no need for you to worry." She tried to push past him, but he blocked her way.

He looked down at her. "But I do. I want to make a suggestion to you. Until Fala is caught, you've got to have someone with you."

She cocked her head to one side and frowned. "What do you mean?"

Mitch pulled his cell phone from his pocket and held it out to her. "Call Gwen. Ask her to stay with you until Fala is caught."

She started to protest, but his words made sense. No matter how brave she tried to appear, she was scared, and Mitch knew it. As she stood there, his eyes boring into hers, she knew he was right. She didn't want to be alone. Tears flooded her eyes. A voice inside her head whispered that he still cared enough to want to protect her.

C.J. nodded. "I think that's a good idea."

NINE

With a sigh C.J. stacked the last plate in the dishwasher and reached for the detergent under the sink. From the direction of her guestroom, where Gwen had taken up residence, C.J. could hear the Saturday morning cartoons. C.J. smiled and shook her head at how much she'd learned about Gwen's likes and dislikes since she'd moved into the spare room. Cartoons were one thing, however, that she would never have suspected from her practical friend.

C.J. could hardly believe a week had passed since the murders. No messages or calls from Fala had arrived all week, and Jimmy Carpenter had not reappeared. She was beginning to feel as if maybe the game were over. Perhaps Mary and Caleb were to be Fala's only victims, but the promise of the riddle still gnawed at the back of her mind. *Four there are,* it said.

One good thing had come out of the past few days, however. The tension between Harley and Michael seemed to have eased somewhat. Caleb's wife, his sole beneficiary, had appointed Caleb's assistant manager to run the car dealership for her, and none of the business's advertising had been pulled from the radio station.

"Can I do anything to help?"

C.J. turned and smiled at Gwen, who stood in the kitchen

door. For the past week her friend hadn't left her side, but today was different. Gwen had to run some personal errands. No matter how much C.J. protested, Gwen had insisted she wouldn't go unless C.J. allowed Mitch to spend the day with her. C.J. wondered if this was Gwen's way of getting the two of them together, but she couldn't be sure.

C.J. had tried not to think about Mitch in the last few days, but it became difficult to ignore her thoughts about him. Until Fala was caught, she'd probably be seeing a lot of him. She would have to be careful not to let his concern for her safety undermine her resolve to keep their relationship in the past.

She sighed. "I don't know why everybody thinks I have to have someone with me all the time. I'm perfectly capable of taking care of myself."

Gwen started to respond, but the doorbell interrupted her. "That must be Mitch. I'll let him in."

Gwen darted from the kitchen. C.J. heard the door open and Gwen's words of greeting to Mitch before she called out. "Hey, C.J., Mitch's here, and I'm leaving. Have a good day."

The front door closed, and C.J. stood in the kitchen. She braced herself for Mitch's entrance. When he stepped through the door, she took a step back to keep from rushing to him. His eyes looked tired, but the smile on his face told her he was as glad to see her as she was to see him.

He held out the morning newspaper to her. "I picked this up in the driveway."

She reached out, took it and laid it on the table. "Thanks."

He pointed to the paper. "There's an article on the front page I thought you might want to see. I read it early this morning and wondered if you had, too. When I saw your newspaper in the driveway, I started to throw it in the trash can, but decided that you might need to know about it."

Puzzled, she sank down at the kitchen table, and Mitch settled into a chair across from her. Opening the paper, she gasped at the bold print that jumped from the top of the page—Talk Show Murderer Still at Large.

She groaned. "They just won't give up, will they?"

Mitch shrugged. "It's news, and that's what sells newspapers."

Her eyes quickly scanned a recap of the events surrounding Mary's and Caleb's murders. The article mentioned the calls and e-mails C.J. had received from Fala. She gritted her teeth at Harley's quote in the article. When asked by a reporter for a statement about C.J.'s contact with the killer, Harley had responded in his typical fashion.

"Did you read Harley's quote?" she snarled.

Mitch nodded.

"I can't believe this."

Harley Martin, producer of *C.J.'s Journal* for WLMT, confirmed the report that a mysterious caller identifying himself as Fala called in twice to talk to C.J., both times threatening a murder. "If you were listening to *C.J.'s Journal,* you heard this Fala tell C.J. she could stop the murders if she'd figure out the riddles that came in some e-mails. According to Fala, there are going to be two more murders."

C.J. threw the paper down on the couch. "I could wring Harley's neck. The less said about this, the better."

Mitch nodded. "Absolutely."

She jumped up from the table and began to pace back and forth in front of the sink. "Every day I wonder if I'm going to hear from Fala. It's driving me crazy. When's it going to stop?"

Mitch stood up and stuck his hands in his pockets. "Soon,

I hope. We have a few leads, but I'm not at liberty to tell you about them. But I do have a request from Chief Stoker for you."

"What does he want?"

"He wants you to come to the station Monday morning. There's something he'd like to discuss with you."

Puzzled, C.J. tilted her head. "Do you know what it is?"

Mitch nodded. "Yes, but I'll let him tell you about it. In the meantime, I'm at your disposal today. What do you have planned?"

C.J. stood up. "I have some errands to run. Are you coming with me?"

"I sure am. With Fala and Jimmy Carpenter both threatening you, I intend to see that you're safe. Where are we going?"

"I have to drop off some clothes at the dry cleaner and then go to the supermarket."

Mitch nodded. "I'm ready anytime you are."

Mitch pushed the cart down the crowded aisle of the grocery store. In front of him, C.J. scanned the shelves for the items on her list. He followed her movements as she bent to lift a bag of flour from a lower shelf and thought back to their conversation at her house.

After a week, Mitch still couldn't make sense of the evidence he and Myra had collected. They'd spent hours discussing the puzzle of the hairs in the victims' hands and the blond woman's presence at the restaurant. She matched the description of the woman with Jimmy Carpenter, but she had been seen with Caleb shortly after Harley left him.

Was she with Harley or Jimmy? Or were all three involved in the murders? If only Mitch knew where to look for the mysterious Didi. So far, the police hadn't been able to come up with her last name. When they did, Mitch wanted to be the one to question her.

He wished he could warn C.J. about his suspicions regarding Harley, but for now that's all they were—suspicions. At the moment it appeared as if Harley might have an alibi for Caleb's murder. When Mitch had questioned Harley about his whereabouts after leaving Justine's, Harley said he had gone to the American Grill and stayed there until it closed two hours later. The staff had backed up his story, but Mitch had seen friends lie for suspects before.

If Harley was involved, then C.J. was too close to a killer. All he could do was warn her about the danger around her and hope she would listen. It seemed, however, that she delighted in opposing him at every turn.

His fingers tightened on the handle of the shopping cart, and he clamped his teeth together. He tried to remember what they'd said to each other the night she broke the engagement. She'd been excited about her show, and he'd told her how dangerous it could become. Suddenly, she'd looked at him with tears in her eyes and said, "I can't be married to a man who wants to manipulate me."

He still reeled from those words. Manipulate? That wasn't what he'd intended at all. He was trying to warn her, but she wouldn't listen. Now they had come to this—two strangers trying to outsmart a sadistic killer.

In an effort to clear his thoughts, he blinked and pulled a bottle of cooking oil from the shelf. "Need any of this?"

She shook her head and walked ahead of him.

He took a deep breath and replaced the bottle. He followed C.J. down the aisle. As she started to turn the corner, she gasped and stopped, frozen in place.

"Hello, there. I'm glad to see you," a familiar voice said.

Mitch's stomach churned at the drawl he knew so well— Pastor Donald, the man he'd wanted to perform their marriage ceremony. She'd opposed him on that, too, saying she wanted to get married by a justice of the peace at the courthouse. He'd tried to change her mind, but she'd been adamant.

As the problems between the two of them escalated, Mitch had sought Pastor Donald's counsel, and he knew the minister prayed for them.

"Mitch," Pastor Donald said, his eyes lighting up, "how good to see you."

Mitch stuck out his hand. "Pastor, fancy meeting you here."

Pastor Donald chuckled. "Well, preachers have to eat, too, and my wife's under the weather today. So I got stuck with the shopping." His gaze darted from Mitch to C.J. "I'm glad to see the two of you together."

C.J. reached into the shopping cart and busied herself rearranging the canned vegetables. "It's not what you think. Mitch is staying close to me because of some rather scary calls to my radio show."

The minister pursed his lips. "The one who says he's a murderer?"

Mitch's eyebrows shot up. "How'd you know about that?"

Pastor Donald shrugged. "I heard the broadcasts." His eyes softened as he glanced back at C.J. "I'm sorry you're going through a difficult time. If there's anything I can do to help you, please let me know. I'm always available to talk."

She straightened her shoulders and took a deep breath. "Thank you, Pastor Donald, but I'm fine." She smiled at Mitch. "I think I'll go over to the produce section. You can join me there when you get through talking."

She strode away, her back stiff. Mitch turned back to the minister. "I'm sorry."

The man's eyes seemed to bore into his soul. "I've been trying to contact you. Since you slip out of church before I get a chance to talk to you, I came by the police station last week, but I didn't catch you."

Mitch sighed. "You warned me about falling in love with an unbeliever, but I wouldn't listen. I guess I just haven't wanted to face you."

Pastor Donald shook his head. "I would never say I told you so, but I would like to help you through a bad time."

Mitch looked in the direction C.J. had gone. "Thanks, but right now she's my main concern. There's a crazy killer loose in this town, and for some reason he's picked her to terrorize."

"Take care of her and yourself. I'll be praying for you."

Mitch nodded as he pushed the cart past the minister. "Thanks."

He hurried toward the produce aisle, silently chastising himself for letting C.J. get away from him. His warnings about staying with him when they'd entered the store didn't seem to have registered. It was going to be impossible to protect her if she insisted on ignoring his precautions.

As he rounded the corner next to a bin of potatoes, he spied her talking to a strange man in front of the lettuce. With a groan, he shook his head in amazement and headed toward C.J., who appeared to be deep in conversation. He rolled his cart to a stop next to her. "I thought I'd lost you."

C.J. handed him a bag of carrots. "I needed some vegetables."

The man laughed and placed a head of lettuce in his cart. "C.J. was helping me with a menu."

Mitch raised his eyebrows. "You know each other?"

The man shook his head. "No. But once she started talking, I recognized her voice. I listen to her show all the time."

C.J. stuck out her hand. "Thanks, Ray. It's good to meet a loyal listener."

He shook her hand, nodded to Mitch and pushed his cart down the aisle. Mitch watched as he headed in the direction of the meat counter, then he turned back to C.J. "Have you ever seen him before?"

"No, but he seemed very nice. He's cooking dinner for his girlfriend tonight and needed some help with what to prepare. I don't think he's been in a kitchen much, and he wants to impress her."

Mitch leaned closer to her and lowered his voice. "You shouldn't be talking to strangers. For all we know Fala could be in this store watching our every move." He glanced in the direction the man had disappeared. "That guy could even be Fala."

Her face paled, and her hand grasped his arm. "I never thought of that." Fear blazed in her wide eyes. "It's so hard to remember that everything has changed in the past few days. I'll be more careful, Mitch. I promise."

He patted her hand. "Good. I just don't want you talking to the wrong person. Stay with me until we're through here, and you'll be fine."

She sniffed and offered him a lopsided smile. "I'm sticking to you like glue until we're back home." They looked into each other's eyes for a moment before she turned away. "I've got everything I need. Let's get out of here."

He followed her as she headed to the checkout counter. His eyes scanned the shoppers they passed. Fala could be among them, watching for a chance to get to her.

You're being paranoid, he told himself. So far Fala had only warned C.J. about the murders, but hadn't actually threatened her. Maybe Mitch was being too protective of her. On the other hand, if the e-mails were to be believed, there were going to be four victims, and she might very well be one of the other two.

Until they knew for sure he wasn't taking any chances. He intended to keep her as close to him as possible.

The warmth from the heater blew upward, sending the cigarette smoke swirling through the interior of the car. Fala, eyes fixed on the entrance to the supermarket, slumped behind the steering wheel. C.J. had already been in there for thirty minutes. What could be taking her so long?

Fala drew on the cigarette, inhaling the smoldering fumes. Strange how the taste of tobacco only satisfied during game time. Months might pass without one, but the moment the game began, the craving emerged once again.

The automatic exit door of the store opened, and C.J. emerged, followed by Mitch, pushing a cart filled with bags. They chatted as they strolled across the parking lot. With eyes closed, Fala chuckled.

I'm here, C.J. Did you see me in the supermarket?

If they only knew. Several times they'd been within a few feet, but they'd never realized it. The old cliché that you can't see the forest for the trees seemed appropriate for C.J. and Mitch. Maybe they were more interested in discovering lost love than in solving the riddles.

"Keep it that way," Fala whispered. "It's not time for you to know. Not yet, but soon."

Mitch loaded the bags in the back of his car and pushed the cart to the return area. C.J. took a step as if to follow, but Mitch waved her to stay.

Hugging her coat around her, she stood alone several feet behind the car. As she watched Mitch's progress, she took a step farther into the street.

Again C.J. was behaving in her predictable manner. Fala chuckled. Foolish girl.

Fala turned on the ignition and the motor roared to life. Hit and run. What could be simpler? Mitch was too far away to stop it. C.J. remained motionless, as if inviting death. The heavy boot pressed against the accelerator. The car eased forward.

The urge to kill welled up with an overpowering desire for more blood. A shiver ran through Fala's body. Game rules that were decided long ago could not be broken. There were other moves to be made before C.J.'s time would come. Fala pulled out of the parking spot and turned in the opposite direction.

TEN

The police station bustled with activity on Monday morning. C.J. sat in a chair behind Mitch's desk and listened to the voices drifting through the hallway. He'd left her here while he went to the chief's office, but he'd been gone a long time. Her fingernails drummed on the desktop. What could be taking so long?

She needed to get to the radio station. What could Chief Stoker want with her? She'd told Mitch and Myra everything she could remember about Mary's murder and Fala's calls and e-mails, and she had work that needed to be done.

Her heart thudded with guilt. How selfish of her to think about her own needs after what had happened to Mary. Mary's murder appeared to be a result of their friendship, and C.J. would never be able to put that from her mind. Then there was Caleb. She'd only met him the night of the broadcast, but his death also seemed to be a direct result of his association with her. Could Fala have known Caleb was going to be on her program, or was his part in the scheme decided while he was being interviewed?

Footsteps in the hall caught her attention, and Mitch hurried into the room, followed by a balding man. She rose as the police chief walked toward her and extended his hand. "Good morning, C.J. I'm sorry to have made you wait. I know you probably need to get to work, so I won't keep you long."

She smiled. "I was glad to come, although I can't imagine what other information I might have for you."

Mitch stood beside his boss and offered him a chair before he glanced in her direction. "I was just bringing the chief up to speed on our progress in the case, and Mary's son-in-law called while I was there."

C.J. sank back down in her chair. "Is Mary's family in town?"

Mitch shook his head. "The shock has been too much for Mary's daughter. She's had to be hospitalized."

"Mary always said Rebecca was in fragile health." Tears sprang to C.J.'s eyes. Mary's conversations about her daughter's bouts with depression had bored C.J. in the past. Now she found herself wishing she could reach out across the miles and wrap Rebecca in her arms. She wiped the tears from her eyes. "What will they do about the house?"

"They've hired a local lawyer to take care of everything. The house was already in the daughter's name, so the lawyer will list it and have all the contents shipped to her."

"What about Otto?" C.J. asked.

The muscle in Mitch's jaw twitched. "They can't take him. They're leaving him with the Humane Society."

The memory of Mary walking the spunky dog about the neighborhood brought fresh tears to C.J.'s eyes. "Oh, Mitch, what if he doesn't get a good home?"

Mitch swallowed. "I'm sure they'll take good care of him."

"But I feel as if he's my responsibility. Can't we do something?"

Mitch pulled up a chair and sat down next to Chief Stoker. "We'll talk about this later. Right now we have something important to discuss with you."

She blinked her tears away, laced her fingers together and propped her arms on the desk. "What is it?"

A sad expression flitted across Chief Stoker's face. "I want you to know that we're doing everything we can to catch this killer. I've had officers investigating around the clock, but so far we've turned up nothing."

C.J. glanced from Mitch to the chief. "What about the e-mails? I thought you'd be able to find out where they came from."

Chief Stoker shook his head and raised his eyebrows. "This Fala is a smart cookie. We thought we could identify the ISP from the messages, but we couldn't."

C.J. frowned. "I'm sorry, but I'm not sure what that is."

Mitch leaned forward. "ISP stands for Internet service provider, and the ISP name is attached to each message that's sent. In this case Fala used a public provider, like in a coffee shop. There's no way to follow the trail."

"But we will catch this killer," Chief Stoker said. "We just have to get the right break. That's where you come in."

C.J. frowned. "Me?"

The chief turned to Mitch before he continued. "We want to monitor your show and goad Fala into calling again. We'll have our equipment set up to trace the call in hopes of finding where the call's coming from."

C.J. thought about that for a few moments. "Have you talked to Harley about this?"

Mitch shook his head. "We wanted to run it by you first. I know you don't want to talk about the murders. But if you went on the radio and blasted Fala for the murders, he might call in again."

She shivered at the thought of having to talk to that monster again. But if it would help to catch Fala, it would be worth it. "I'm willing to do it. Harley will love it because it'll probably attract more listeners." She took a deep breath. "Okay, when do we set up the trace?"

"Tonight," Mitch said. "We'll be right there with you."

C.J. pushed up from the desk. "In that case, I'd better get to work."

Mitch stood. "I'll drive you, then we'll be back later to get everything set."

She nodded and walked around the desk. For the first time a trace of hope glimmered inside her. Maybe tonight Fala would fall into their trap, and the nightmare would be over. Mitch walked to the door and held it for her to precede him down the hall.

He fell in step beside her. Myra, studying several sheets of paper, ambled into the hall through a doorway. She smiled as she saw Mitch, but the corners of her mouth drooped a little when she caught sight of C.J.

"Good morning, C.J.," she said. "How're you holding up?"

C.J. straightened her shoulders and smiled. "I'm fine."

Myra returned her focus to Mitch. "I have some things to go over with you."

He took C.J.'s arm and steered her toward the door. "I'm driving C.J. to work, but I'll be right back."

Myra smiled. "Come to my office. I'll have a pot of coffee ready."

C.J.'s heart plummeted at the familiarity in Myra's voice and the way her eyes devoured Mitch. Myra was waiting for Mitch to rebound into her arms, and there was nothing C.J. could do to stop it.

A helpless feeling overwhelmed her. Even though she'd known how Myra felt, C.J. had never seriously considered that Mitch might return those feelings. C.J.'s heart pounded as if it was shattering into little pieces, and she almost groaned aloud at the thought hammering in her head: *you've turned your back on the only man you will ever love.*

Fifteen minutes until showtime. C.J. sat in the broadcast booth and watched several computer technicians from the police department set up electronic equipment in the next room. Harley bustled about, laughing and chatting with the men. Chief Stoker stood to the side and offered comments from time to time.

Mitch entered and sat down next to her. He watched the activity for a few moments before he spoke. "It looks like everything's just about ready."

She nodded. "I checked with Harley. He has the pre-recorded tape ready to roll."

Mitch said, "I'm glad. Your idea to cut away from the program was a good one. How will that work?"

"When they see his number, Harley will switch me off and turn on the tape. It says that we're experiencing some technical difficulties at the moment. Then music will play. That way our listeners won't hear what Fala has to say."

Mitch nodded. "Good. We don't want to encourage him any more than we have to."

She took a deep breath. "We've given that killer enough airtime already. There's no need to scare the citizens of Oxford any more. The minute his call comes in, I'll be talking to Fala without it being broadcast."

"What if Fala's listening and knows he's not on the radio?" Mitch asked.

She sighed. "I guess we'll deal with that when the time comes."

He glanced back at the men in the next room. "I hope this works."

Her gaze followed his. She sat still for a moment before she turned to him. "Have you ever been involved in tracing a call before?"

"A few times." His forehead wrinkled. "I remember a few years ago a college student was attacked and raped when she came home one night. The rapist got away, but he would call her and threaten to come back. We finally traced his calls, but she was terrified until we caught him."

"That must have been awful."

"It was. She was a beautiful girl, and that creep turned her into a paranoid woman, old beyond her years." His voice held an edge, and pain flickered in his eyes.

C.J. picked up her headphones and rubbed the band with her thumb. "I've wanted to ask you something for a long time."

He tilted his head to the side. "What?"

"Why didn't you ever talk to me about your cases?"

His eyes grew wide. "I didn't want you to know about the violence and evil I saw every day. I wanted to shield you from all that."

She looked into his eyes. "But sometimes when we were together you'd brood until the silence would almost drive me crazy. I thought you didn't want me to help you get through the rough times."

He swallowed. "It wasn't that. I didn't want you touched by the things I saw."

"I see." She glanced down at the headphones and cleared her throat. "Well, evil sure had a way of finding me. What can I expect tonight?"

Mitch pointed to the men on the other side of the window. "If Fala calls in, Marty and Bob will be ready to trace the call. I've worked with these guys before, and they're the best in our technology department. If Fala uses a regular phone, they'll need you to keep talking so they can trace the number." He shrugged his shoulders. "Of course, he may use a cell phone. If that's the case, they'll have to use their global positioning software to pinpoint the location."

C.J.'s eyes grew wide. "They can do that?"

"Technology is making advances every day. Every cell phone now has a chip embedded inside it that allows it to be located." He moved his chair nearer to the console. "We have no idea whether Fala's using a landline or not. We're just trying to cover all bases."

C.J. nodded and pointed to an extra set of headphones. "Wear those so you can hear everything."

In the next room Harley began the countdown. C.J.'s fingers trembled as she pulled the mic closer. The thought of talking to Fala again sent fear rushing through her, but she had to do this. They had to find this killer before some other innocent victim suffered Mary's and Caleb's fates.

Two hours later, during the break for the news, Mitch sat hunched over the console, the legal pad in front of him covered with doodles. An array of listeners had called in to voice their concerns about life in Oxford—the main topic tonight being the killer walking the streets.

In the next room Chief Stoker took a seat next to Marty and Bob. Harley entered the room with a fresh pot of coffee and poured some in their empty cups. Chief Stoker shook his head and placed his hand over his mug. Mitch chuckled to himself. He wondered how much coffee had been consumed during the last two hours.

Mitch peered through the window separating the two rooms and studied Harley. Even though Harley appeared to have an alibi for the night of Caleb's murder, Mitch hadn't completely eliminated him from the list of suspects. Harley, apparently unaware that he was under suspicion, laughed and joked with the men around him.

C.J. was about to enter the last leg of the show, and no call had arrived from Fala, even though C.J.'s comments to listeners had offered a clear challenge to the killer. Maybe Fala wasn't listening tonight. Mitch glanced back at Harley. Or maybe the reason Fala hadn't called was because he knew exactly what was taking place inside the radio station.

With no word during the last week, Mitch was beginning to worry that this case might be growing cold. He'd seen unsolved murders disappear into the dusty files of the department in the past, but he didn't want this one to end like that.

The door to the broadcast room opened, and C.J. walked in. "I like to walk around during the breaks. There aren't many chances to do that during the program."

He glanced at the clock. "Is it almost time to begin?"

She nodded and clamped the headphones back on. "Yeah. I don't understand why I haven't heard from Fala. Maybe I need to blast him even more. He's got to call in soon, or this is going to be a wasted night."

He knew she was referring to the program, but still her words stung a little. Sitting next to her had given him pleasure. She was so different when she was speaking into the microphone, so poised and sure of herself. Not at all like the angry woman who'd ignored her need for God and had accused him of trying to run her life.

He swallowed and watched her as she busied herself choosing a mini disc. As long as that wedge existed between them, there was no hope of their getting back together. He had to find Fala and then get out of her life.

"Welcome back. We're on the air once again and waiting to hear from you." Her words startled him and brought him out of his thoughts.

The caller screen beside her lit up, and he watched as C.J. connected with the first one. He settled back in his chair and crossed his arms. Nothing showing up yet. It looked like the last segment was not going to produce anything more than the first two had.

"Welcome to *C.J.'s Journal,* Frank," she said.

"Thanks for takin' my call," a man's voice replied.

She leaned forward and spoke into the mic. "What can I do for you tonight?"

"Well," he said, "You've already had some folks call in 'bout this killer in Oxford. But I was just wonderin' if the cops got any leads yet."

C.J.'s gaze went to the men in the next room. "I know they're working on the case, but they're not yet ready to make an arrest."

"I've been scared to let my kids out of the house, and we've been sleepin' with a gun next to the bed."

"I certainly understand your concern, Frank, but maybe the police will put an end to this crazy lunatic soon."

"Maybe so," Frank said.

C.J. took a deep breath. "This murderer *will* be stopped, Frank. I promise you that. He's a demented psychopath with no remorse for what he's done. I guess the only word to describe him is *insane.*" She glanced at Mitch and swallowed. "A person like that can't stay hidden forever. He's going to make a mistake, and when he does, he's going to pay a high price for his crimes."

"I hope it won't be long 'fore they get 'im. I want my kids to be safe." The man's voice cracked on the last words.

"Oh, they'll find him. He thinks he's so smart, but his sick mind is no match for the police. This creep is going to be caught." She pulled the microphone closer, her eyes sparkling with an excitement that Mitch had never seen before. "You know, when I think about it, he's not only crazy, but he's stupid. What makes him think he can commit horrible murders and not make a mistake? And he made one when he decided to go on a killing spree in Oxford. Understand this, Fala. Your days are numbered. Get ready, because retribution is coming."

"I sure hope you're right, C.J."

"I do, too, Frank. Thanks for calling."

She disconnected the call, sank back in her chair and breathed a sigh of relief. In the next room Chief Stoker and Harley nodded their heads and smiled. Mitch reached across and squeezed her arm.

She turned and gave him a weak smile. She had given Fala the bait. Now they had to see if he would respond.

About thirty minutes later, Mitch noticed movements from the men in the next room. Chief Stoker jumped from his chair and hovered over Marty and Bob. A big grin covered Harley's face. He flashed a victory sign with his fingers before flipping the switch to the prerecorded tape.

Mitch saw a private number on the caller screen. C.J.'s face paled, and her fingers fumbled to bring the microphone closer. She reached out, grasped his arm and closed her eyes for a moment. Taking a deep breath, she leaned forward.

"Good evening, caller. What's on your mind tonight?"

A soft chuckle came over the phone. "Really, C.J. Must you be so formal with me? You were certainly calling me all kinds of names a few minutes ago."

Mitch's eyes widened in amazement at the transformation he saw take place. Her body relaxed, and she leaned forward, her arms folded on the console, and spoke as if she were chatting with an old friend. "I wondered how long it would take to hear from you again."

An eerie chuckle rattled over the line. "Missed me, did you?"

She pursed her lips. "Oh, I don't think that's the word. How could I miss someone who evidently has no conscience and enjoys hurting people?"

"Why, C.J., you surprised me tonight." Sarcasm dripped from the words. Mitch searched his mind, trying to identify the familiar tone of the voice, but he couldn't place it. He pulled his attention back to what Fala was saying. "You're beginning to play very aggressively."

C.J. frowned. "Maybe because I've never been involved with someone so obviously disturbed as you. Why would you want to hurt someone as sweet as Mary Warren? And why Caleb Lawrence? What did either of them ever do to you?"

"Why, nothing." The voice held a hint of surprise. "They were just pawns in the game. You were supposed to defend them better by solving the riddles."

C.J. clenched her fists and rubbed them on the console. "There you go again with your crazy game talk. Would you have stopped if I had figured out the clues?"

Fala laughed. "Well, we'll never know the answer to that now, will we?"

"But I just don't get it. Why did you involve me in this sadistic nightmare?"

"Because you're the chosen one, my dear. I thought you'd be a better player, but you've disappointed me. You have to defend your position if you want to stop the killings."

Mitch glanced in the next room where Marty and Bob still sat bent over their equipment. He turned back to her and mouthed for her to keep Fala on the line. They hadn't established a location yet.

She cleared her throat and spoke again. "Have you seen the newspapers? You're making quite a name for yourself with your public threats and confessions to murder."

"I've enjoyed the publicity." Fala sighed. "I suppose by this time everybody in Oxford and the surrounding area knows my name. The good citizens of the city are locking their doors and looking over their shoulders, wondering if they're next."

At that moment Chief Stoker gave them the thumbs-up signal. Mitch felt a surge of excitement, and turned to look at

C.J. Her face beamed. Electricity seemed to crackle in the air as she reached out and grabbed Mitch's hand. Her body relaxed, and a smile curled her lips.

"Well, enjoy your fifteen minutes of fame, because it won't last. When the police get you—and, believe me, they will—you're going to pay for what you've done. And I'm going to be there to see that you get what you deserve."

Fala's chuckle turned to a laugh. "You amuse me, C.J. Before I go, though, I do have one more thing to say. Be sure and check your e-mail."

The line clicked, and the phone went dead.

C.J. and Mitch pulled their headphones off and dropped them on the console. C.J. jumped up and turned as if to run from the room. Mitch started to follow, but the door burst open and Chief Stoker rushed in. "We couldn't get a trace on the number. It was a prepaid cell phone, but Bob got a location."

"Where was he?" Mitch said.

"Out by the Cumberland River Bridge. I have units on the way there now." He nodded to Mitch. "I'm on my way. Want to go with me?"

Mitch grabbed his jacket off the chair. "Oh, yeah, do I ever." He turned back to C.J. "You stay here until I get back. You'll be safe. There are officers downstairs."

She nodded, her face white. "Good luck. I hope you catch him."

"Me, too," he said as he turned and rushed out of the room.

His hand went to the gun attached to his belt. Maybe by the time they got to the river, the first officers on the scene would have Fala in custody. He could hardly wait to see who they caught in their trap tonight.

C.J. ran from the broadcast booth toward her office. She could hear Mitch and Chief Stoker's footsteps on the stairs as they headed toward the front door. Maybe they'd find Fala, but she had to see what the latest e-mail message said.

The thought propelled her down the hall and into the room where so much of her day was spent. She flipped on the light as she entered and then rushed to the computer. She sank into her chair and reached for the computer mouse.

When her e-mail messages came into view, Fala's name stood out from all the others as if in bold print. With shaking fingers, C.J. opened the message and read Fala's latest riddle.

Two are gone and two remain
But one of them will soon have pain.
Watch them now like giant flames.
Begging you to guess their names.
Fala

She sat there for a few minutes, staring at the screen. "Hurry, Mitch," she whispered. "Stop him before it's too late."

The dark waves rippled against the shore of the Cumberland River and splashed the rocks along the bank. Usually a few barges plowed the murky depths, but not tonight. Only the hoot of an owl from a tree in the forest covering the steep banks broke the silence. The glowing lights from the bridge that spanned the river sent reflected beams dancing across the smooth surface far below.

C.J. had behaved just as expected. And why wouldn't she, with all those policemen and their equipment around? He'd laughed at the sight of the boxes being unloaded from the police cars and taken inside WLMT. You'd think they'd be smart enough to do it in a secretive way, not right out in the open for anyone to see.

But then the Oxford Police Department didn't have any

great brains on the force. Maybe they'd learn something from trying to solve their latest case.

The watch's face glowed in the dark. It wouldn't be long now. They were probably already approaching the bridge. Time to go. Fala's arm arced and heaved the cell phone toward the river. A splash pierced the quiet.

Who did those fools think they were dealing with? One of the rules of the game required a different prepaid cell phone for each call.

"And so the third phone joins the fish," Fala whispered to the night.

No time to linger. Another move had to be made. Death waited.

Fala turned and ran through the woods. In the distance, blue lights flashed. In a few minutes footsteps would be crashing through the forest.

Fala jumped in the car, and the motor purred to life. "You're too late again."

ELEVEN

C.J. walked from her office and entered the broadcast booth next to hers. The men who'd used the tracking equipment were still busy dismantling the devices and putting them back into cases. Harley stood over them, watching their movements. They looked up as she came into the booth.

"Any news yet?"

The man Mitch had called Marty smiled up at her. "Not yet. But it's a long way out to the river. The first officers should have gotten there quickly, but they're probably still searching."

She rubbed her hands together. "Do you think they'll call?"

Bob rose to his feet. "My guess is we'll hear from Mitch as soon as he knows anything. It shouldn't be much longer. But there is a problem."

"What?"

"The signal from the phone died."

C.J. looked from one to the other. "What does that mean?"

Bob shrugged his shoulders. "We don't know. Maybe the phone's been destroyed so we can't follow its signal. Maybe it means nothing."

Marty closed the cases containing their equipment. "At this point all we know for sure is that the global positioning signal abruptly disappeared. We need to get back to the station and see what we can figure out, but the officers downstairs won't leave until you do. So you and Mr. Martin can take it easy until you get some word."

C.J. held out her hand to the men. "I will, and thank you for all you've done to help me tonight."

Marty shook her hand. "We were just doing our job, but we sure would like to catch this guy."

Bob shifted the case he held to his left hand and reached toward her with his right. "Yeah, especially since he's targeted Oxford's favorite radio star."

She smiled at the men again. "I appreciate that."

They lifted the last cases and headed out the door. Their footsteps echoed through the empty corridor as they ambled toward the stairway. When the sound disappeared, she turned back to Harley, who stood with his hands in his pockets and a smile on his face.

"You did a good job tonight," he said.

She pulled out a chair from the table where Marty and Bob had sat and dropped down into it. "Thanks. I don't really remember what I said to Fala. I just knew I had to keep the conversation going so they could try to locate where the call was coming from."

Harley nodded. "And you did it right." He sat down in a chair next to her and clasped his hands in front of him on the table. "I know you get upset with me sometimes because you think I push too much, but it's only because you have that special quality so many radio personalities lack."

C.J. tilted her head and frowned at him. "What's that?"

"You're completely at ease on the air. You make it sound like you're sitting in your kitchen listening to your best friend's problems over a cup of coffee. You don't lose your cool with any of the callers, and the sincerity in your voice helps them feel you really care about them. That's priceless in radio. There's no telling where you could end up." Harley shrugged. "Maybe even on TV."

She laughed and patted his arm. "That's sweet, Harley, but I doubt I'll ever leave WLMT unless Mr. Cunningham asks me to. I love this station and the town."

Harley nodded. "Yeah, it does grow on you. I kinda like it myself." He looked at his watch and sighed. "I've got a lot of work to do before I leave tonight. Want to wait in my office with me until Mitch gets back?"

"I'll head back to my desk." She swallowed. "I checked my messages. I had another one from Fala."

Harley shoved his hands in his pockets and smiled. "Don't worry about it. Maybe by this time the police already have Fala in custody. If they do, that message won't mean a thing."

The thought eased her mind, and she smiled. "I hope you're right, but I can't believe it's almost over." Excitement filled her as she walked to the door. Maybe it *would* be over soon. "I'll wait for Mitch in my office, but we'll pop in to see you before we leave."

Harley switched off the lights as they stepped into the hallway. "See you later," he called over his shoulder.

C.J. walked back to her office and sat down behind the desk. Within minutes she heard footsteps on the stairway. She tensed as the footsteps approachd her office and she breathed a sigh of relief when Mitch walked in the door.

The expression on his face told her what she wanted to know before she asked. The excitement she'd felt a few minutes before died. Dread at what he would say replaced it. She wrapped her fingers around the arms of the chair, slumped back in it and spoke in a hollow voice. "They didn't catch him, did they?"

Mitch shook his head and settled into the chair across from her. "There was nobody near the river when the officers got there."

Her hands began to shake, and she tightened her fingers. "Marty and Bob said the phone signal disappeared."

Mitch rubbed his hand across the back of his neck. "Yeah. Fala's not taking any chances. That phone's probably at the bottom of the river. That would account for the sudden signal failure."

C.J.'s eyes grew wide. "Will you have divers look for it?"

Mitch shook his head. "It would be like looking for a needle in a haystack. We don't know where Fala was along the riverbank or even if the phone was thrown in the river. With the currents out there, we'd never find it. Besides it's just a theory at this point."

"I was so sure we'd catch him tonight." C.J. swallowed. "Mitch, there's another e-mail."

Mitch sucked in his breath. "Fala said to check your messages. Let me see it."

He walked around the desk and stood looking over her shoulder as she pulled up the latest e-mail. He read the words silently and then walked back and sank down in a chair. He sat there, rubbing his eyes.

"Another one. When is this going to stop?"

"I don't know. I don't understand why Fala picked me. I feel so helpless."

Mitch smiled at her. "You were great on the radio with him. I couldn't have kept my composure the way you did. I was really proud of you."

She lowered her eyelids, her face growing warmer by the minute. "Thank you, Mitch. That means a lot to me."

He stood up and checked his watch. "I'll get in touch with headquarters and alert them about this, but I think I'd better get you home now. The guys downstairs left when I came in, but what about Harley? Is he still here?"

"Yeah," Harley said from the door. "I just came down to check on C.J. I have some budget problems I'm working on. I'll be here for hours yet, but you two go on. Lock the downstairs door on your way out."

C.J. turned toward Harley. "Are you sure you want to stay here alone?"

Harley stepped into the room. "I can't go home yet. I have an early-morning meeting with Mr. Cunningham."

C.J. frowned. "Is there a problem?"

Harley pushed his glasses up on his nose and stuck his hands in his pockets. "Mr. Cunningham wants to go over my expenses in the morning. I think Michael may have been talking to him." Harley took a deep breath. "But there's nothing for you to worry about. Your show's doing great, and the ratings are climbing every day."

An uneasy feeling rippled through her. "Does your problem with Mr. Cunningham have anything to do with my show?"

Harley couldn't meet her gaze. "What makes you think that?"

His evasive answer told her she had guessed right. "Because you violated our policy the first time you put Fala on the air. You promised me you'd never take a private number or any kind of threatening call. But you put Fala through, and that was a deadly mistake."

"But I thought it was just some nut. I didn't know it would go this far," Harley whined.

She clenched her fists and took a step toward him. "You should have been more careful. You put a lot of people in danger. Two are dead, and now Fala's threatening a third one."

Harley took a step backward and looked from her to Mitch. His chin quivered a little, and his teeth bit down on his lip. After a moment he nodded. "You're right. This is my fault."

He paused, and C.J. knew he was waiting for her to protest, but she held her tongue.

His shoulders slumped. He sighed, and C.J. knew he realized he would get no sympathy from her tonight. "I wanted this job so much I thought if I made you the most popular show on radio, I'd be set for a long time. I wasn't about to let anybody or anything stop me from getting what I wanted."

"I've always told you I appreciated what you've done for me. But we have a responsibility to the public, and I think you forgot that."

He swallowed, and a tear rolled from the corner of his eye. "From the very beginning you told me our listeners are real people with problems. I didn't think of them that way. I treated them like they were nothing but a means to an end."

"Instead of remembering that, you chose to give a lunatic a sounding board to brag about his crimes. I don't think the ratings were worth the lives of two people," C.J. said.

Harley took a step toward her. "You may not believe me, but I've felt guilty over Mary's and Caleb's deaths. Now I've got another person to worry about."

C.J. glanced back at her computer. "And I have no idea who it is." Her voice trembled as she thought of Fala stalking some unwary soul.

"I was just trying to make your show a hit." His eyes pleaded with her to understand.

"Well, you went about it the wrong way. All we can do now is hope that Fala makes a mistake and the police catch him," C.J. replied.

Mitch held out a hand to C.J. "And we will, Harley. Now why don't we get out of here? Maybe by tomorrow our tech guys will have come up with something we overlooked." He picked up C.J.'s coat and held it as she slipped her arms into it. "We'll be in touch tomorrow about what our next move will be."

Harley nodded. "Sure, Mitch." He took a step toward her. "And C.J., please believe me. I never meant to hurt you."

C.J.'s emotions warred within her. Harley had been good to her. He'd given her the opportunity with the show, but he had violated their agreement when he put the first calls from Fala through. Her conversations with a murderer had taken their toll on her emotions, and she doubted if she would ever feel safe again.

She buttoned her coat. "Harley, tomorrow after you meet with Mr. Cunningham, I think we need to sit down and have a long talk."

He nodded. "Okay. I'll see you in the morning."

C.J. watched as Harley turned and shuffled out the door. His step wasn't as jaunty as usual. She hoped Harley hadn't been too reckless in his determination to make her show a success. If something caused management to cancel her program, she didn't know what she would do. She'd lost Mitch, and a crazy killer was now harassing her. That was enough to deal with without losing the only thing she had left.

She turned to tell Mitch she was ready to leave, but the words froze in her throat at what she saw in his eyes. Instead of the I-told-you-so attitude she might have expected six weeks ago, she detected something quite different—sympathy, understanding and a glimmer of what might be love. Perhaps this was a sign that she and Mitch could still salvage their relationship. She started to speak, but before she did he blinked, and a veil clouded what moments before had sparked a new hope in her.

TWELVE

C.J. didn't think she'd closed her eyes all night. When Mitch brought her home, she and Gwen had sat up until the early-morning hours talking about Harley and his meeting with Mr. Cunningham. Once she'd gone to bed, she'd lain there, replaying the events of the night. Sleep hadn't come, and now her body protested against getting out of bed.

She tiptoed past the bedroom where Gwen slept and crept into the kitchen. A cup of coffee was what she needed. As she waited for the pot to brew, she went outside to get the paper. She'd just picked it up when Adam stepped out of his house and waved to her.

"C.J.," he called. "Want to run with me this morning?"

She and Adam often shared their early-morning run together, but today she didn't think her body would survive the two-mile route.

"Not today, but thanks anyway," she called.

Adam jogged across the street and stopped in front of her. "I have a lot of work waiting, and I may not get to the gym. Thought I'd just do the neighborhood route. Are you sure you don't want to come along?"

She thought of Gwen still sleeping. "I'd better not. I'm going to wait for Gwen to wake up."

Adam smiled. "Did you girls stay up late talking again?"

"Yeah, we did." She slipped the rubber band from the rolled up newspaper and smiled as a thought struck her. "Hey, why don't you join us for dinner tonight after I get home from the broadcast? I can stop for Chinese takeout."

Adam kicked at a rock that lay by his foot and glanced up at C.J. "Gwen told me Mitch has been bringing you home after your broadcasts. Don't you think it might be a good idea to invite him, too?"

C.J. frowned and started to protest. "Adam, I don't think…"

"Aw, come on, C.J. The guy has been knocking himself out for you. The least you could do is invite him to have dinner with friends."

She swallowed back a retort and sighed. "I guess you're right. I'll ask him."

Adam smiled. "Good. And who knows? You may even enjoy yourself."

C.J. laughed and headed toward the house. "Maybe so."

Adam waved and jogged down the street. She smiled to herself as she entered the front door. Gwen and Adam seemed to be hitting it off, and she was glad. Gwen had often confided how lonely she was, and then Adam had entered her life. It warmed her heart to see her friend blossoming into a woman in love.

By the time C.J. returned to the kitchen, the coffee was ready. As she poured a cup, she glanced at the clock. Seven a.m. Perhaps she should wake Gwen. She was usually up by this time, but after their long chat session she probably needed some extra rest. She'd give her a few more minutes.

C.J. picked up the newspaper and went into the den, but paused in the doorway, her gaze resting on the computer. The very thought of the messages awaiting her sent chills down her spine.

"Not another e-mail from Fala," she whispered to the empty room. Not after last night.

She took a step forward and tossed the newspaper on the couch. The computer drew her across the room, and she inched toward it, easing into the desk chair. Taking a deep breath, she opened the e-mail program and scanned the sender names that came into view. Her fingers on the mouse shook at the sight of a new message from Fala.

"No. Please, no." The words rasped from her dry throat. *Just hit Delete,* her mind argued. That was impossible. She had to know. Hesitantly, she opened the message and stared at the words.

And now there's three, aren't you sad?
Your guessing skills are really bad.
He hoped to make your show the best,
But you have laid his plans to rest.
Fala

The shrill ring of the telephone jolted Mitch from a deep sleep. For a moment he couldn't get his bearings. Then he realized he was in his own bed. Groggy, he reached for the cordless phone.

"Hello."

"Mitch! Mitch!"

He bolted from the bed and headed toward the dresser where his gun lay. "C.J., what's the matter?" he yelled. His feet skidded on the hardwood floor, and he reached for the wall to steady himself.

"I have another e-mail from Fala. He's killed again." Her shrill voice pierced his ear.

He winced and pulled the phone away for a moment. "Calm down and tell me what it said."

Mitch listened as she read the e-mail to him. He leaned against the dresser and bit his lip as the meaning of the words penetrated his now-awake mind. "Oh, C.J., do you think…"

"Think?" she wailed. "He's talking about Harley. Do something. Get some officers out to his house right away."

"What's his address?"

"4915 Griffin Street."

He reached for his cell phone. "C.J., I'm going to put this phone down while I call the station on my cell phone. Don't hang up. I'll be back on the line shortly."

"Hurry, Mitch," she sobbed.

Jennie, the dispatcher, answered on the first ring. "Oxford Police Department."

"Jennie, Mitch Harmon here. I think we may have another murder." After relating all the information to her, he closed the cell phone and picked up the cordless phone again. "C.J., you still there?"

"Did they know anything?"

"No. They're going to check his house and the radio station. Jennie said she'd call when they have any news. We don't know for sure that Fala meant Harley. We'll have to wait and see."

He heard her sob. "He meant Harley all right. But why? Harley can be obnoxious sometimes, but he really does have a good heart."

"Now don't get upset before we know anything for sure. It shouldn't take too long, depending on where the officers were patrolling."

He'd never felt so helpless in his life. The woman he loved was in agony, and their only connection was a telephone line. How he wished he could reach out, pull her into his arms and tell her how much he loved her. Now wasn't the time, though.

Finally, his cell phone rang. "Hello."

"Mitch," Jennie's voice said. "The officers found Harley Martin's body in his garage. He'd been dead for some time."

"Thanks, Jennie. I'll get right over there."

He closed the phone and spoke into the cordless. "C.J., they found Harley's body in his garage."

"No!" she screamed. "Harley didn't deserve this. What kind of monster is Fala?"

All Mitch could do was to shake his head in disbelief. The man he'd suspected of being Fala now had died at his hands. "I don't know. We've never had such a sadistic killer in Oxford before. We *will* catch Fala, C.J. I promise you that."

"Please, you have to. I'm afraid I'm going to lose my mind if I have to endure much more of this."

He heard a sudden rustling and knew that C.J. must be hurrying through her house. "Gwen's still asleep," she said. "I've got to wake her and tell her what's happened. Then we need to get to the station. I can't imagine what it's going to be like there when this news breaks."

"Stay close to Gwen today, and I'll talk to you when I know more."

"Okay, be careful, Mitch."

A click sounded on the line as the connection was broken. Mitch punched the off button and placed the handset back on the cradle. He closed his eyes and massaged his temples with his fingers. He was tired of e-mails and murders. Sometimes he wished he'd never chosen this profession. Then he wouldn't be exposed to the horrible things that people did to each other.

With a sigh, he sank to his knees by his bed. "Oh, God, give me strength to face another murder scene. Give me wisdom to find the answers that will put an end to this violence."

He rose, knowing that whatever he must face, God would be there with him. He could only imagine how the garage at

Harley's house would look. Mitch's stomach churned at the thought of what Harley had suffered at the hands of Fala. Three people were now dead, but the first e-mail said there would be four. He shivered at the thought that Fala wasn't through yet.

An hour later C.J. and Gwen sat alongside Michael Grayson in the station manager's office at the radio station. Don Cunningham leaned back in the swivel chair behind his desk and stared at them with tired eyes. Every time C.J. had seen him at the station, he'd been impeccably dressed. But not today. He had the look of someone who'd pulled on the first clothes he could find, and his gray hair stuck out in back as if it hadn't been brushed. He tapped his desk with a pencil he held in his right hand.

C.J. looked at Gwen's pale face out of the corner of her eye and swallowed. They'd never been called into the station manager's office before, but today was no ordinary day.

After a few minutes Mr. Cunningham spoke. "This is a tragic morning for our station. I'm in shock over Harley's death."

C.J. nodded. "We all are."

Mr. Cunningham pursed his lips and wrinkled his forehead as if he were deep in thought. After a few moments he cleared his throat. "Even though we've experienced this horrible tragedy, I still have to look out for the best interests of the station."

C.J.'s heart fluttered. There was something besides sorrow over an employee's death in Mr. Cunningham's eyes. She leaned forward and studied her boss more closely. "I understand, and let me assure you that Gwen and I will do everything we can to handle Harley's responsibilities until you decide who will fill his job."

He glanced at Michael Grayson. "Well, that's what I wanted to discuss with you. Michael and I have been talking this morning. In light of the events of last night, I think we need to cancel *C.J.'s Journal* for the time being."

C.J. sat up straight in her chair. "Mr. Cunningham, it'll be difficult without Harley, but we can do it."

Michael Grayson raised his hand to his mouth and muffled a soft cough. The station manager nodded to him. Michael turned to face C.J. "It's not just a matter of Harley's death. I've had several calls over the last few days from your sponsors. They don't want to be associated with a program that gives a killer publicity."

Gwen slid forward to the edge of her chair. "That's not fair. C.J. had nothing to do with that. Harley was the one who allowed Fala on the air."

Mr. Cunningham held up his hand as if to signal an end to the discussion. "That may be, but the damage has been done. If you don't have sponsors, you don't have a show. For the time being, the show is canceled." His gaze swept all three. "Is that clear?"

Michael Grayson stood up and nodded. "Quite."

C.J. grasped the arms of her chair and pushed up. "Will we be able to resume broadcasting when Fala is caught?"

Don Cunningham picked up some papers. He didn't look up, an indication that he considered the meeting over. "I'll let you know. For now I suppose you two can consider yourself on paid leave. Michael, will you help them gather up whatever they want to take with them?"

Michael smiled. "I'll be happy to."

Michael held out his hand to indicate that it was time for them to leave. The cuff of his Armani shirt slipped up to reveal the leather band of his diamond-studded watch. C.J. had seen that watch every day for weeks, but somehow today it seemed out of place.

Her gaze trailed upward to the pink shirt and the expensive silk tie. How could Michael afford to dress so well on his salary? Maybe there was more to him than any of them had ever guessed.

She and Gwen preceded him into the hallway. When he closed the door, the smirk on his face grew larger. Infuriated, C.J. advanced on him. "Did you get what you wanted, Michael?"

He looked from one to the other, his expression never changing. "I warned you. Now you can suffer the consequences."

C.J. stared after him as he walked down the hall. "He enjoyed every minute of that. Maybe his problem wasn't with Harley. Maybe it was me."

An uneasy feeling settled in the pit of her stomach. She'd never realized that Michael disliked her so, but it had become painfully obvious in the last few minutes. The thought that troubled her was that he wasn't the only one. Fala didn't like her, either. Could it be a coincidence, or were Michael and Fala the same person? That would explain how Fala knew so much about her. She swallowed back the fear that Fala had been right down the hall from her office for months, watching every move she made.

Mitch watched from inside the garage as the coroner's technicians loaded Harley's body into an ambulance. Jeff Parker, the coroner, stopped in front of him. "Do you have any questions before we leave, Detective?"

Mitch shook his head. "I think Sergeant Borden's given us everything we need."

Jeff waved to the attendant who climbed in on the driver's side of the ambulance and then headed to his car. Mitch walked to the corner of the house and watched as they drove down the driveway from the garage at the back of the house.

Fala had picked the perfect spot for a murder. With the

garage secluded from view, Fala probably waited for Harley in the shadows, unobserved by anyone passing by.

Myra and Sergeant Borden approached Mitch, and he turned to face them. "It looks like the same method as Mary's and Caleb's murders," Mitch said.

Myra nodded. "Yeah. A blond hair in the victim's hand, but this time his truck is missing."

Mitch slipped the notepad he held back in his pocket. "Bloody handprints at Mary's house, Caleb's knife missing and now Harley's truck. There has to be a connection, but I don't see it."

Sergeant Borden pulled off the latex gloves he wore, turning them inside out, and stuffed them in his pocket. "Don't worry. You'll find it."

"I hope you're right," Mitch said.

In his time on the police force, Mitch had never felt more helpless with a case than with this one. The newspapers were calling for Fala to be caught, and the citizens of Oxford were frightened over where he would strike next.

Mitch had to find the link to these murders. He mentally checked off the clues—bloody handprints, a knife, a truck, a blond hair and C.J. The last one hit him like a punch in the stomach. For some unknown reason, Fala had chosen to put her in the middle of the worst murder spree in the history of Oxford.

Chills raced up Mitch's spine as he wondered what Fala had planned next for C.J. He straightened his shoulders and took a deep breath as a renewed determination spread through him. Taking a deep breath, he strode toward the garage and whatever clues it held. He had to find Fala. No way was he going to let C.J. end up as the next victim.

"If you want to get to her," Mitch muttered, "you'll have to kill me first."

* * *

Empty cartons from the Chinese restaurant littered the table. Having dinner with Adam and Gwen had been just what C.J. needed, but the mood had been somber throughout the meal. Harley's death had been the main topic of conversation, and she'd only mentioned the cancellation of her program once during the whole time. She wanted to discuss it more, but she could tell by the relieved look on Mitch's face that he was happy that she was off the air.

The thought of not talking to Fala offered her some comfort, but there were still the e-mails. Once or twice she'd almost sent a reply to the messages, but she couldn't bring herself to get any more involved in this sick game than she already was.

Across the table Adam gestured to the last egg roll. "Who's going to get that?"

Gwen raised an eyebrow and grinned at him. "Well, not you. You've had more than your share tonight."

He laughed and patted his stomach. "I guess I've had enough to eat." He turned to C.J. "How about you?"

She shook her head. "Nothing else for me." She smiled and glanced from Adam to Gwen. "I'm glad we've been together tonight. I think we all needed this time to cope with Harley's death."

Adam nodded. "I didn't know Harley very well. Met him a few times with Gwen, and I liked him. It's hard to believe all this has happened to people we know. First Mary and now Harley." He reached over and squeezed Gwen's hand. "Of course, we shouldn't forget Caleb Lawrence. I didn't know him at all."

Mitch rose and stepped over to the coffeepot on the cabinet. "None of us did. I can't figure out the connection between the victims."

"It's me," C.J. said, her voice cracking. "They all knew me."

Adam frowned and leaned forward. "But there has to be some other link between the three of them. I'm sure the police will figure it out and catch him. Right, Mitch?"

Mitch took a sip of his coffee. "Oh, yeah. It's just a matter of time." He sat back down at the table and wrapped his fingers around the mug. "I keep thinking that Jimmy Carpenter must play into all of this in some way. Especially after he and his girlfriend threatened C.J. in the radio station parking lot."

"What?" Adam and Gwen spoke at once.

Gwen turned wide eyes to C.J. "You didn't tell me that."

C.J. hadn't wanted to talk about that night, but now she couldn't keep it secret any longer. "It happened the night it snowed. Jimmy warned me to stop mentioning him on the air."

"There was also a car registered to Jimmy in front of her house," Mitch added.

Adam slumped back in his chair, his eyes wide with surprise. "Maybe Mary was right to be frightened of drug dealers moving into our neighborhood. Do you think Jimmy Carpenter could have killed her?"

"Right now we don't have any evidence to connect him with the crimes, but I can't help but believe he's involved in some way." Before Mitch could say any more, his cell phone rang. He unclipped it from his belt and frowned at the caller ID. "I wonder who this is. I'll take it in the other room."

He jumped up from the table and strode from the room toward the den. C.J. strained to hear what he was saying, but he was too far away.

Gwen began to gather up the dishes. C.J. reached out to her. "Don't bother. It won't take me but a few minutes to clean up. Let's enjoy being together."

Gwen checked her watch. "I didn't realize how late it was."

In the distance a dog barked, and C.J. cocked her head to listen. She wondered how many times she'd heard Otto's bark from the yard next door. Where was he tonight? Did he have a new home where he was loved?

C.J. leaned back and sighed. "I've been thinking about getting a dog."

Adam stood up, a grim expression on his face. "Maybe you need to get what Gwen has—a gun."

C.J.'s mouth dropped open. "When did you get a gun?"

Gwen smiled sheepishly at Adam. "After Mary's murder, Adam insisted that I get one for protection. He helped me pick it out, and we've been going to the shooting range to practice."

C.J. tilted her head to the side. "I don't think I want a gun. Maybe a dog is a better choice for me."

"Have you thought about what breed you'd like to get?" Gwen said.

C.J. reached across the table and pulled Gwen's and Adam's dishes toward her. She stacked them on her plate before she looked up. "I thought maybe I'd take Otto if no one's adopted him yet."

"Otto?" Gwen asked. "Why would you want him?"

C.J. shrugged. "I feel as if I owe it to Mary to take care of her dog. I think about him all the time and wonder if he's being cared for."

"Of course he is. He's with the Humane Society people," Gwen said.

C.J. stood up. "Well, it's just a thought."

Gwen leaned forward and propped her elbows on the table. "When it comes to Fala, I'll take my gun over a dog any day."

Adam put his arm around Gwen. "Even if you are armed and dangerous, you're still beautiful."

Gwen's face beamed with happiness as she stared up at him. "Thank you, kind sir."

Adam stood and stretched. "Tell Mitch I'll talk to him later. And thanks for dinner." He pulled Gwen to her feet and put his arm around her. "Want to walk me to the door?"

They headed toward the front of the house, and C.J. could hear their whispers as they bid each other good-night. When Gwen reappeared in the kitchen, a glow lit her face. She smiled at C.J. "I think I'll go to my bedroom and leave you and Mitch alone for a while. See you in the morning."

C.J. nodded. "Sleep well."

She sat alone in the kitchen as Mitch entered from the hallway. "Where are Adam and Gwen?"

"Adam left, and Gwen's in the bedroom. Adam said he'd talk to you later."

Mitch nodded, but she could tell his thoughts were far away.

C.J. poured another cup of coffee for both of them and sat down at the table. He sank into a chair across from her. She raised her cup slowly to her lips. "Who was that on the phone?"

"Dean Harwell. He's an undercover drug agent."

"What did he want with you?"

Mitch hesitated before answering. "Usually I wouldn't tell you about my work, but you're too involved in this case not to know what's happening."

She leaned forward, her heart beating. "Does this have something to do with Jimmy Carpenter?"

Mitch nodded. "Dean's had an apartment building under surveillance. He thinks it's Jimmy's base of operations. They're going to raid it in the morning, and he's asked me to come along."

Fear churned in her stomach. "That could be dangerous."

He picked up his coffee cup and looked at her over the rim. "Just another day at work."

Holding her mug, C.J.'s fingers trembled. Ever since Fala had entered her life, she'd come to understand the kinds of evil Mitch faced. It frightened her. She couldn't stand it if something happened to him.

She set her cup down and reached across the table. He stared at her for a moment before his fingers inched out and wrapped around hers.

His thumb rubbed across her knuckles and ignited a warm glow inside her. She grasped his fingers tighter and smiled. How she had missed this. For a few minutes she wanted to forget Fala and all the evil he'd brought into her life.

Instead she wanted to bask in the memories of days gone by when she felt so alive and free to tell Mitch how much she loved him. The pulse in her neck throbbed, and she wondered if Mitch could hear its faint chant. I love you, I love you, it whispered over and over.

THIRTEEN

Mitch stopped outside the police station the next morning and watched the day-shift patrol officers drive away. Not too many years ago he'd been one of them and knew how quickly a routine call could turn into a life-threatening situation. He waved and breathed a prayer for their safety.

A rush of adrenaline shot through him at the thought. The only thing better than catching Fala would be seeing Jimmy Carpenter's drug operation crumble. He and Myra had followed up many leads in the past, but they had all fallen flat. This new information offered the first break in months. Maybe the raid would even uncover Fala's identity.

Once inside his office, Mitch turned on his computer. When it booted, he opened the file he'd been keeping on the murders. The victims, how they'd died, the similarities and differences in the crime scene, the blond hairs—it was all there. The discrepancies in Fala's actions still puzzled him. Why handprints at Mary's, a knife taken from Caleb and Harley's truck stolen?

As he read the notes again, a sudden thought struck him. Bill Diamond headed the local field office of the FBI. He'd once mentioned a facility the agency had in Quantico, Virginia, where information was stored on cases that might have been committed by the same person. He struggled to recall the name and snapped his fingers as it popped into his head—the National Center for the Analysis of Violent Crime.

Fala mentioned on the radio that he had killed before. If he'd done that, he might be a serial killer with an FBI file of past crimes.

Grabbing a telephone directory, Mitch looked up the number for Bill's office and dialed. Within minutes he was deep in conversation with the agent, telling him everything he knew about the three murders.

"Do you think you could check this out for me, Bill?"

"Sure, Mitch," came the response. "Shoot me an e-mail with everything you've got, and I'll send it in. Don't know how long it will take to get a reply, but they'll run it through the system."

The first glimmer of hope bubbled up in him. This could be just what he needed to catch Fala. "Thanks. Give me a call when you know anything. We're ready to get this killer off the streets."

"Will do."

"Wait a minute," Mitch called out. "Let me give you my cell phone number."

Mitch recited the number and sat there after he hung up. He wanted to catch Fala more than any other criminal he'd pursued, but catching him did have a downside. Once Fala was behind bars, Mitch wouldn't be seeing C.J. anymore.

The memory of C.J.'s fingers laced with his the night before returned. It had felt so good just to touch her again. For a few moments they had connected the way they'd done in the past, and he'd been happier than he'd been in months. He was afraid to read too much into the fact that she'd initiated the contact, but it had given him an indication that C.J. might still have feelings for him. Maybe there was still a chance for them.

Before he could pursue a reunion, he had to find Fala. With a sigh he directed his attention back to the information he'd assembled about the murders.

For the next few minutes he perused the file, attached it to an e-mail and sent it to Bill. He'd just hit Send when a voice broke the silence. "Good morning. What are you doing here so early?"

Myra stood in the doorway. "I was hoping you'd get here. Dean Harwell's got a drug raid this morning and asked me to go along. Do you want to come?"

She stepped forward and stopped in front of his desk. "Sure. When?"

"Right now," a voice behind her said.

Myra turned as Dean walked into the office. As often as he'd seen Dean in his undercover disguise, Mitch still did a double take each time they met. In his baggy jeans and dirty sweatshirt, he looked like he'd spent the night sleeping on the street. A long ponytail hung down his back, and a red sweatband circled the upper part of his head. Gold studs pierced his ears. His mouth, barely visible through the moustache and beard that sprouted on his face, twitched at Myra's intense look.

"You're not used to working with a good-looking guy, are you?" he teased as he looked from her to Mitch.

She laughed. "I'm sorry. I was just trying to see the police officer I know underneath all that hair."

He nodded. "Well, where I go, you gotta fit in, and I sure wouldn't if I dressed like your partner."

Mitch chuckled and came around the desk. "We appreciate your letting us go along this morning. Jimmy Carpenter is a person of interest in the murder cases we're working on. What do we need to know before we leave?"

Dean pulled a piece of paper from his pocket. "I have the search warrant. So we're all set. The apartment building we're going to is a rundown place in the Orange Hills area of town, Foley Street."

Mitch and Myra exchanged glances. He gave a low whistle.

"That's a rough part of town. The residents down there don't take kindly to police cruisers on their turf."

Dean laughed. "We're going in unmarked cars, but there'll be backup waiting for my signal. Maybe we'll be lucky and take them by surprise." He frowned and studied the two detectives for a moment. "'Course the lookouts will know who we are soon as you get out of the car. Nobody down there dresses like that."

Mitch grinned and said, "We'd better change into the clothes we keep in our lockers for Dumpster searches."

Myra nodded, and they hurried from the room. They were back within minutes, dressed in jeans and sweatshirts. Mitch faced Dean and spread his arms. "Now I think we're ready."

Dean tossed his car keys to Mitch and motioned to the door. "You drive. I'm too excited. I've spent a year building a case against Jimmy Carpenter, and I'm ready to bring him down."

Mitch and Myra checked the guns they wore and followed Dean from the building. Mitch gazed up into the clear sky as he opened the car door. It was a perfect day to bust a drug ring.

C.J. and Gwen, unsure how to occupy their time on suspension, settled in front of the television in the den. The talk shows all covered the same story this morning—a rock star's divorce from one of the world's most beautiful models. They sipped coffee as they followed the latest events on the celebrity scene.

Gwen pulled her feet up underneath her and sighed. "This story would probably have produced several calls on tonight's show."

C.J. nodded. "Yeah. Too bad we won't be on the air."

Gwen set her cup on the coffee table in front of the couch and frowned. "I don't understand it. Why would our sponsors all decide to drop the program at the same time?"

C.J.'s eyebrows crinkled on her forehead. "I was thinking the same thing last night." She sat silent for a moment. "I thought we had such a good relationship with all of them. You'd think at least one of them would talk to me personally instead of relaying a message through Michael Grayson."

Gwen shrugged. "I don't know. They might have been ashamed to face you if they were going to pull the plug on your program."

C.J. stood up and began to pace up and down the den. "Maybe, but I can't believe Mr. Higgins wouldn't call me. He's told me so many times that his advertising on our show had practically doubled his auto parts sales."

Gwen stood up and stretched. "I know Wendi at the beauty salon has been pleased. I saw her about two months ago. She said she was staying booked all the time. Her new customers told her they all heard about her salon on your program."

C.J. walked over to her desk and pulled a notepad and pen from a drawer. "I'm going to make a list of my sponsors." They sat down on the couch as C.J. began to write. "Okay, there's Higgins Auto Parts, Wendi's Salon, Patterson's Realty and Forsythe's Quick Stop. That's all of them, isn't it?"

Gwen nodded.

C.J.'s mouth drew into a grim line. "I'll go in the kitchen and call Mr. Higgins and Mrs. Patterson on my cell phone. You can use the one in here to reach Wendi and Mr. Forsythe. Let's tell them we were a little surprised at their pulling our advertising and ask what we've done that caused them to do it."

"It can't hurt to ask them what it would take for them to return as sponsors."

C.J. jumped up. "I'll come back when I've finished talking with my two."

Fifteen minutes later C.J. entered the den just as Gwen was placing the handset back on the hook. Gwen glanced up at C.J., her eyes dark with anger. "You're not going to believe what I found out."

C.J. plopped down on the couch and hit the coffee table with the notebook in her hand. "Probably the same thing I heard."

They looked at each other for a moment, then spoke in unison. "Michael."

C.J. nodded. "Mr. Higgins and Mrs. Patterson both told me Michael Grayson started calling about a month ago hinting that *C.J.'s Journal* was losing its audience. He said their advertising would benefit them more if they sponsored another program. They said he was very apologetic that they were sponsoring a show that was dropping in the ratings and assured them he would place them in better spots."

"That's the same thing he told Wendi and Mr. Forsythe." Gwen banged the arm of the couch with her fists. "That snake!" she yelled. "He lied to Mr. Cunningham to get him to cancel our show. Why would he do such a thing?"

C.J. stood up. "I don't know, but I'm going to find out. I think we need to pay a visit to Mr. Cunningham."

Gwen's eyes grew wide as she rose beside C.J. "Mitch told us not to leave the house. He'll be angry if he finds out."

C.J. waved her hand in dismissal. "This is a matter of saving our jobs, Gwen. We have to go to the station and get this straightened out." She smiled and looped her arm through her friend's as she guided her toward the door. "Besides, you have a gun. There's no need for me to be afraid as long as I'm with my pistol-packing friend."

Gwen shook her head. "I don't know about this."

C.J. sighed in resignation. "Oh, if you're going to be that way, why don't you call Adam while I'm getting my coat? If he's not too busy painting, maybe he can ride with us."

Gwen smiled. "Now that's an idea. Why didn't I think of that?"

C.J. laughed and ran toward her bedroom. Suddenly, she felt as if there was hope she could save her career. She'd been terribly depressed ever since the meeting in Mr. Cunningham's office, but a new energy surged through her.

It puzzled C.J. why Michael Grayson wanted her off the air. Michael had to answer for his actions, and she wasn't going to rest until he did.

Hoping the unmarked car went unnoticed by the neighborhood residents, Mitch drove slowly down Allen Street. He'd made several arrests in the area and knew that violence could erupt at the slightest provocation.

Run-down houses and apartment buildings lined the street. Junked cars sat in several of the yards, and large dogs slept on many stoops. With the temperature in the twenties today, there weren't many people outside. He was glad about that. Word spread like wildfire when police were spotted in the area.

"Pull over here." Dean's voice startled him.

"Why?"

"The apartment building on Foley is just around the corner. It's been condemned, and for the most part it's deserted. Homeless people sleep there lots of nights. Jimmy moves from place to place, but he's used this one for about six months now."

"How'd you find it?" Myra asked.

"One of my street buddies told me about it. I've been buying from them for several months now. There's a guy that keeps a lookout on the front steps. I've gotten to know him." Dean opened the car door. "I'm going to get out here and walk. Give me five minutes before you drive up."

Mitch nodded. "Be careful."

"I'm wired for sound. I'll be giving instructions to the guys who're waiting two streets over to back me up. You'll know how things are going."

Dean stepped out of the car and staggered down the street. Mitch chuckled at the transformation that took place in the officer. He looked just like one of the city's homeless who searched each day for another drug or alcohol fix.

Mitch glanced at his watch as Dean disappeared around the corner. Dean's voice came over the radio. "One guard—Tootie they call him—lounging on the steps. Usually there's two. The other one must be upstairs. Move in to cover the back of the building so Finis doesn't get away."

"Got it," a voice replied.

For a few moments, there was no sound, then Dean spoke again. "Hey, man, how ya doin'?"

"If it ain't old Chester. Where ya been, dude?" a deep voice drawled.

"Hangin' around. But I need some stuff."

"He's talking to the guy on the steps," Myra said.

Mitch nodded.

"Whacha need, man?"

"Somethin' good for a candy bowl party tonight. Oxy, V, Number Nine. Whatever ya got. And I wouldn't mind gettin' a little nose candy for myself."

There was a moment of silence. Mitch's heart pounded. What if the guy didn't bite?

"Man, I doan know."

"Come on." Dean paused for a moment. "Whadda ya say, Tootie?"

"Well, maybe. Where this here party gonna be?"

Dean laughed. "I cain't tell ya that. Them dudes wouldn't take to me givin' away their location."

"Big party?"

"I think so. They tryin' to bring in a bunch of high school kids on this one." Dean hesitated a moment. "Tell ya what, Tootie. I could pass the word along to some of 'em where the best stuff in town can be bought."

"Hmmm, think you could?"

"Yeah, man. Just get me the stuff, and I'll tell 'em how to connect with you. You still hang out down on the corner of Main and Church?"

Tootie laughed. "Yeah, Church. Ain't that funny?"

"Cool, man," Dean said.

"Well, I guess I can help out. Finis, he's upstairs. C'mon."

"Wait a minute. I gotta have me some nose candy now. I can't wait."

The guard's laughter crackled on the radio. "You anxious, huh? We'll git it upstairs."

"Come on, Tootie. I need it now. Just give me one snort, and I'll be ready to do business."

"Give me the money first."

There was a momentary silence, and Mitch could imagine Dean digging in his pockets for some money. "Okay, here's what you charged me the last time," Dean said.

Tootie laughed. "You remember real good. And here's what you need."

There was a rustling, then a cry of surprise. "What ya doin', man?"

"You're under arrest for drug dealing. You have the right to remain silent…"

Mitch pressed the accelerator as Dean continued to read the man his rights. The car rounded the corner, and he screeched to a stop in front of a dilapidated two-story brick building. Cardboard covered several of the windows where the glass had been broken. Dean stood on the second of a tall flight of steps, his gun pressed into the back of a short, stocky man. Mitch and Myra were out of the vehicle as soon as it stopped, and Mitch ran forward to cuff the suspect.

Suddenly, police cars with wailing sirens filled the streets, and officers jumped from inside. "Get this one in the car," Dean yelled.

As the officers led the guard to a waiting car, Dean headed up the steps, Mitch and Myra right behind him. The front door of the building burst open, and a burly man charged out, his gun leveled at Mitch. A look of surprise crossed his face as he stared at the three guns pointed at him. Before he could turn to run, several uniformed officers appeared behind him.

"Drop the gun!" one of them shouted.

The burly man glared at Dean before he dropped his weapon and raised his hands. Hatred flashed in his eyes as the officers pulled his arms down and handcuffed him. He spat toward Dean, the glob landing on the front of Dean's shirt. "A narc," he snarled. "I shoulda killed you the first time I laid eyes on you."

Dean pulled a bandanna from his pocket and wiped his shirt. "Too bad. You missed your chance."

The officers grabbed the man's arms, led him down the steps, and placed him in the back of a cruiser. Myra turned back to Dean. "What now?"

He pointed toward the building. "The guys are going through the apartment now. Want to go up and see what they've found?"

"Sure."

The three of them started up the steps, but turned at the roar of an approaching motorcycle. The bike, with a man and woman aboard it, skidded to a stop, made a U-turn and sped away. The man was hunched over the handlebars, and the woman, her hair blowing in the wind, had her arms wrapped around his waist.

"That's Jimmy Carpenter and his girlfriend," Dean cried.

"Quick! Get in the car!" Mitch yelled.

They scrambled down the steps and jumped into the car they'd driven to the raid. Mitch floored the accelerator and switched on the siren as they roared after the fleeing couple.

Mitch's fingers gripped the steering wheel, his mouth tightening in a thin line at the sight of the woman's long blond hair—just like the strands found in the murder victims' hands. He clenched his teeth and concentrated on overtaking the motorcycle disappearing in the distance.

This was their chance to put away the biggest drug dealer in Oxford. Not only that, but Jimmy had to answer to Mitch for threatening C.J. in the radio station parking lot. It would only be better if they could prove that Jimmy Carpenter was Fala. No way was Mitch going to let him get away.

He glanced down at the speedometer needle as they sped through the streets of Oxford, but he didn't let up on the accelerator. From the backseat he could hear Myra yelling at him, but he tuned her voice out.

A bicycle ridden by a young boy appeared to his right from a side street. The boy, unaware of the police car bearing down on him, gazed after the speeding motorcycle and pedaled into the path of the cruiser.

"Mitch!" Myra screamed. "Watch out!"

Mitch jerked the steering wheel to the left and careened around the bicycle just before they collided. He glanced in the rearview mirror and gave a sigh of relief at the sight of the boy standing by his bike and surrounded by people.

Dean, who'd braced himself for a collision, straightened in his seat and shook his head. "That was a close one. Maybe you'd better slow down."

Mitch shook his head. "I can't let Jimmy Carpenter get away. I can't."

FOURTEEN

C.J. and Gwen sat across the desk from Don Cunningham in his office. The station manager, his bushy eyebrows drawn down across his nose, stared at them. He rocked back in his swivel chair and tapped the pencil in his right hand on the desk.

C.J. glanced at Gwen out of the corner of her eye. Thanks to Adam, the hesitancy Gwen exhibited at home turned to intense determination the closer they got to the station. All the way he'd encouraged Gwen to stand her ground. Michael Grayson had been devious, he reminded her, and deserved whatever he got. He recited all her abilities and told her any station would be glad to have such a dedicated employee. Right before they entered the office, he gave her a quick hug and told her he'd be just outside.

Now they waited for Mr. Cunningham's response to what they'd told him. He glanced from one to the other before he leaned forward and took a deep breath. "You understand you've made some serious allegations against Michael?"

C.J. nodded. "Yes, sir. But it's very easy for you to check out. Call the sponsors and talk to them so you can figure out who's telling the truth."

"And then what?"

Gwen leaned forward. "Mr. Cunningham, we've worked

hard to make *C.J.'s Journal* one of the best shows on WLMT. We want to find out why Michael set out to sabotage our program. He never made any secret of his dislike for Harley, but we had no idea those feelings extended to us."

The station manager frowned. "Harley had some problems. Had them before he ever came here. But I still liked the guy. He didn't deserve what happened to him. I knew he and Michael didn't get along, but I thought it was just the normal tension that comes from working closely together."

C.J. shook her head. "I think it was more than that. Michael was livid the night Caleb Lawrence was on the show. He even attacked Harley when Caleb threatened to pull his advertising."

"I didn't know he'd crossed that line." He sat still for a moment, his fingers drumming on the desk, and then he stood up. "Tell you what. I'll check this out. I'll talk to the sponsors, then to Michael. I'll decide how we need to proceed, and I'll let you know."

C.J. and Gwen stood up. "Thank you, Mr. Cunningham. We appreciate that. There's just one more thing," C.J. said.

"What?"

She put her hand on Gwen's arm. "Gwen is one of the hardest-working employees you have. She had nothing to do with Fala or Caleb Lawrence's interview. I'm to blame for all of it. Even if you decide not to reinstate my show, I hope you'll rehire Gwen."

Gwen looked utterly startled. "Oh, C.J., that's so nice of you." She narrowed her eyes and faced Mr. Cunningham. "If you don't put C.J. back on the air, you're making a big mistake. I know WREM would snap her up in a heartbeat."

Don Cunningham chuckled. "I'll be in touch. Don't do anything drastic until I sort this mess out."

His words offered C.J. the first glimmer of hope she'd had for the reinstatement of their program since its suspension.

She could hardly contain her excitement. "Thank you for seeing us. We'll look forward to hearing from you."

As they walked out of the office, Adam jumped up from the chair in the hallway and rushed over. "So what happened?"

"We don't know," Gwen said. "He's going to talk to the sponsors and get back to us."

Adam stepped between them and put an arm around each of them. "Great. Now what say we go get a cup of coffee to celebrate?"

Gwen looked up at him. "Don't you have some work to do?"

He shrugged. "Well, I'm trying to finish that piece my client in Atlanta commissioned, but I can work on that later. I'd much rather spend time with you girls."

C.J. shook her head. "No, you've done enough just bringing us down here." She glanced from one to the other. "But there is one more thing I'd like to do before we go home."

Adam raised an eyebrow. "What?"

C.J. took a deep breath and slipped the strap of her purse on her shoulder. "Go to the shelter to pick up Otto."

"Oh, C.J., are you sure?" Gwen asked.

"I am. I called this morning and talked to the staff. The family who adopted Otto brought him back yesterday. He hasn't bonded with anybody they've tried." She took a deep breath and reached for Gwen's hand. "I'm afraid they may put him to sleep if I don't do something. I still feel guilty over Mary's death, and I can't add guilt over what might happen to Otto to that."

Gwen wrapped both hands around C.J.'s. "Mary's death wasn't your fault."

C.J. swallowed back the tears. "I have to do this, Gwen."

Adam threw back his head and laughed. "Then it's off to the shelter for us. Otto is coming home with you girls, and I'm going to finish my painting."

Gwen stared at C.J. for a moment before she hugged her, then turned back to Adam. "Remember, you promised to cook dinner for me as soon as you completed that painting."

His gaze flitted over her face. "It shouldn't take too much longer. When I'm through with it, we'll celebrate with a fancy dinner. I may even find a special bone for Otto."

They laughed and headed for the stairs. C.J.'s eyes were drawn to the closed door of her office as they passed. Her heart longed to go inside and sit down among the familiar surroundings, but that wasn't possible yet. Maybe soon, if Mr. Cunningham allowed her to come back. But coming back to the station and her broadcast would be much easier if she didn't have to worry about Fala. She could only hope Mitch would catch him soon.

From the backseat of the police car, Myra reached out and grabbed Mitch's shoulder. "Don't let him get away!"

Mitch bit down on his bottom lip and pressed the accelerator. Jimmy Carpenter's motorcycle skimmed along the streets, weaving in and out of traffic. Even with the flashing blue light Dean had put on top of the car and the wailing siren, pedestrians and other drivers were causing problems by not yielding the right of way. They'd be lucky if someone didn't end up getting hurt.

From the other side of the front seat, Dean spoke into his radio. "Suspect and an unidentified woman on a motorcycle traveling south on Merchant Way, headed toward the Cumberland River Bridge. If you apprehend, approach with caution. He may be armed."

Behind them Mitch could hear the wail of other sirens. "Better have dispatch alert the Benford County sheriff. Tell them we're in hot pursuit of a suspect moving toward them by way of the bridge."

Dean relayed the message, then fixed his sights on the motorcycle. "You're doing great, Mitch."

Fear knotted in the pit of Mitch's stomach as the speedometer inched higher. *God, keep us and all the other motorists we meet safe,* he prayed.

"You're gaining on him!" Myra yelled.

Dean pulled his gun and rolled the window down. "Get a little closer. I'll take a shot at their tire."

Mitch swallowed and tightened his grip on the steering wheel as Dean pushed his head and shoulders through the window's opening. The distance between the car and the motorcycle closed up. Just a few more feet, and Dean would be within firing range.

Suddenly, Mitch's eyes grew wide. "Look out, Dean," he yelled. "He has a gun."

Jimmy Carpenter twisted in his seat and fired. Mitch swerved, hoping to evade the bullet. Dean ducked back inside the car. "That was close."

The woman behind Jimmy turned, a gun in her hand, as well. "They're both armed!" Myra cried.

Bullets flew past the car as the two of them fired. The front fender blasted open as a gunshot tore into it. "I gotta do something about this," Dean said, pushing up in his seat. He leaned out the window and fired in rapid succession.

The woman slumped forward. "I think you hit her," Mitch yelled.

For a moment the motorcycle slowed. Mitch watched in disbelief as Jimmy pried the woman's arms from around his waist and pushed her off the back of the bike. Her body bounced across the asphalt and landed in the grass beside the road.

Mitch pulled to a stop, and Myra bounded from the car. "I'll take care of her. Get Jimmy."

Mitch stomped on the accelerator, and the car leaped

forward. Less than a mile away, the bridge that spanned the Cumberland River came into view. They had to overtake Jimmy before they lost him in the next county.

The motorcycle slowed as it approached the bridge. Mitch smiled at the sight in the distance. Patrol cars, their lights flashing, approached from the other direction. Jimmy Carpenter had nowhere to go.

Dean leaned out the window and fired once more, and the bullet stuck the back tire of the bike. The motorcycle turned on its side and skidded in the gravel beside the highway. The minute it came to a stop, Jimmy Carpenter was on his feet and running toward the bridge.

Mitch screeched the car to a halt and then he and Dean jumped out. Mitch pulled his gun and aimed. "Halt! Police!" he yelled, but the man gave no heed.

Jimmy ran to the center of the bridge, climbed on the railing and turned to face his pursuers. Cursing, he pointed his gun at Mitch. The pistol in Mitch's hand jerked as he pulled the trigger. With a cry Jimmy fell forward, his arms and legs spread-eagled as he sailed through the air. With a loud splash he crashed into the muddy water far below.

For a moment his body floated, facedown and arms stretched out, on top of the water. Then it slowly sank beneath the surface.

Preparing to jump in, Mitch jerked his jacket off and grabbed a foothold on the railing, but Dean's hand on his arm restrained him. "No, Mitch. That water is freezing, and the currents are swift here. Nobody could live after a fall like that."

Mitch shook his head. "But he may be Fala. I can't prove he's the murderer if I can't question him."

Dean's grip increased. "He's gone. Maybe his girlfriend made it. Let's go see."

Mitch looked down at the surging river once more. Jimmy Carpenter's body was nowhere in sight.

Disappointment surged through Mitch. He tried to tell himself that Fala had just fallen to his death, but there was no way to be sure. If the killings stopped, then he'd know that Jimmy Carpenter was indeed the murderer, and that C.J. would be safe. Until that happened, all he could do was wait and see if Fala struck again.

Ever since C.J. and Gwen had returned from the radio station, C.J. had had difficulty keeping her mind on Gwen's conversation. Her thoughts kept returning to Mitch and why he hadn't called. It had been hours since he left to meet Dean Harwell earlier in the morning. She willed the phone on the kitchen counter to ring.

"What do you think?" Gwen said.

C.J. frowned at her friend. "I'm sorry, Gwen. What did you say?"

"I said, do you think we'll hear from Mr. Cunningham today?"

She shrugged, picked up her lunch dishes and carried them to the sink. "I don't know. I hope he doesn't make us wait too long before we know something."

Gwen crunched on a potato chip and nodded. "Me, too."

C.J. leaned against the counter and crossed her arms. "I still get furious every time I think about Michael. Even if Mr. Cunningham doesn't take us back, I'm going to confront Michael about this."

Gwen rose and placed her dishes in the sink. "I'll be right there with you."

The shrill ring of the telephone startled C.J., and she reached for the receiver before it could ring a second time. Her heart pounded as she spoke. "Hello."

"C.J., this is Mitch."

Her legs weakened from the relief flooding through her,

and she sagged into the kitchen chair. She'd never been so glad to hear anyone's voice. He was all right. That was the most important thing at the moment.

"Mitch, I've been worried. I thought you would never call."

"Have you really been worried about me?"

His soft voice warmed her. She wished she could tell him how much he meant to her, but fear of his rejection kept her from voicing the words. "I have. Tell me what happened."

"It's a long story. I'm at the hospital now, but I'll come by your house as soon as I can."

"Hospital?" she gasped. She jumped to her feet. If he was hurt, she had to go to him and beg his forgiveness for how she'd treated him. "Are you hurt?"

"No, I'm fine," he reassured her. "I'm waiting to see the doctor about the condition of Jimmy's girlfriend. She was injured. Myra and I want to question her as soon as she's conscious."

Her hand tightened on the telephone. "What about Jimmy?"

"We think he's dead, but we haven't been able to find his body."

New fear at what Mitch must have faced assailed her. She closed her eyes and bit down on her bottom lip. "But you're all right?"

He chuckled. "I'm fine. I'll tell you all about it when I get there."

In the background C.J. could hear someone whispering. "Who's that?"

"It's Myra. She says the doctor is coming out to talk to us. I'll be there as soon as I can. Is Gwen still with you?"

"She's here."

"Good. I'll fill you in later. Bye."

"Goodbye." C.J. held the phone for a few moments before she replaced it in the cradle.

Gwen's wide eyes stared at her. "I couldn't tell what he was saying. Why is he at the hospital?"

"Waiting to question Jimmy's girlfriend." The phone rang again, and C.J. reached for it. "Mitch?"

"No, this is Don Cunningham," a voice said.

C.J. grasped Gwen's hand. "Mr. Cunningham, I'd just hung up from talking with Mitch. I thought he was calling back."

There was a pause on the line and then the sound of a soft cough. "C.J., I've talked with all your sponsors. They told me the same thing you did."

C.J. squeezed Gwen's hand and nodded. "I'm glad you found out we were telling the truth."

"I've also talked with Michael. I'll spare you the details of that conversation. I wanted you to know that this matter isn't over yet. I have some other things I want to check out, but beginning next Monday your show is back on the air. We'll make announcements the rest of this week that the program is temporarily off the air due to the untimely death of Harley Martin, but that we will resume on Monday in the same time slot with a new producer."

She thought she would burst with happiness. "That's wonderful. Gwen's here with me. I'll tell her the good news."

"She's there? I was going to call her, but I can talk to her now."

C.J. handed the phone to Gwen. "He wants to speak to you."

Gwen put her hand over the mouthpiece. Her face turned white. "Do you think he's going to fire me because of how I talked to him in his office?"

C.J. shook her head. "I don't know. Just talk to him."

Gwen gulped and straightened her shoulders. "H-hello, Mr. Cunningham."

C.J. watched Gwen's face as she listened to the station manager. As the minutes passed the color returned to her cheeks, and her mouth widened into a smile. She nodded from time to time and murmured her agreement. Finally, a big grin flashed across her face. "Thank you for having faith in me. I'll do a good job for you."

Anxiously waiting to hear what was being said on the other end of the line, C.J. shifted her weight from foot to foot. When Gwen hung up, C.J. grabbed her hand. "Tell me what he said."

Tears stood in Gwen's eyes. "I can't believe it. He asked me to be your producer. He's giving me Harley's job."

Speechless, C.J. stared at her friend. Then they threw their arms around each other, jumped up and down and yelled at the top of their lungs.

As if the thought hit them at the same time, they stopped and stared at each other. Tears glistened in Gwen's eyes. "I shouldn't be so happy. I only have this job because of Harley's death."

C.J. blinked back her tears and smiled. "But Harley would be happy to know you're taking his place."

Gwen's chin trembled, and she turned away. "I think I want to be alone for a while."

C.J. reached for her, but Gwen slipped past her and headed to the bedroom. C.J. eased back into her chair, propped her elbows on the table and covered her face with her hands. The good news about her job seemed unimportant when weighed against the murders of Mary, Caleb and Harley.

She would give it up if she could only bring them back. That wasn't possible, and there was no guarantee that Fala wouldn't strike again.

FIFTEEN

After Dr. Compton told Mitch and Myra that Jimmy Carpenter's girlfriend, whose real name was Deidre Preston, according to her driver's license, had come through her surgery fine, they went to talk to her. Fortunately for her, the bullet tore right through her shoulder and the doctor didn't think there would be any permanent damage. Dr. Compton continued to monitor her condition as the detectives entered the room.

The young woman, probably in her mid-twenties, lay on a bed inside a glassed-in cubicle in the emergency room, her eyes closed. Her blond hair looked like a frame around her pale face in the way it fanned across the pillow. Her chest moved up and down in a steady rhythm with each breath. Mitch checked out the bedside monitors that beeped in the quiet room. Blood pressure and oxygen level seemed good, and her heartbeat seemed regular. Lying underneath the covers, she looked small and frail, not at all like the woman who had fired a gun at them from the back of a motorcycle.

Mitch stepped forward. "I'm Detective Mitch Harmon, and this is my partner, Detective Myra Summers."

Fear flashed in her eyes, and she squirmed as if to sit up. A frown crossed her face, and she glanced down at her right leg. The sheet covering it moved as she struggled to move. "What's wrong with my leg?"

The doctor gently pushed her down in the bed. "Don't move."

Myra leaned over her. "We have you restrained, Didi. You're wearing a leg cuff with a handcuff attached. It's fastened to the bed."

Didi's eyes grew wider, and tears rolled down her cheeks. "Am I under arrest?"

Myra leaned over her. "You are under arrest for attempted murder of a policeman. You have the right to remain silent. Anything you say can and will be used against you in a court of law. You have the right to have an attorney present during questioning. If you cannot afford an attorney, one will be appointed for you."

Didi's tongue licked at her lips. "Do I need a lawyer?"

Myra stared down at her. "That's for you to determine. You're entitled to have one with you when we question you whether you've broken the law or not."

Didi's lips drew across her teeth in a straight line. "I ain't done nothin' wrong. I don't need no lawyer."

Myra looked up at Mitch, and he nodded for her to continue. "That's not necessarily true. We saw you fire a gun at police officers. We know Jimmy Carpenter was dealing drugs, and you were with him."

Didi's eyes shot angry darts at Myra. "Yeah, I was with him. He took real good care of me, didn't he? Threw me right off the back of his bike." She gritted her teeth. "When I see him, I'm gonna make him pay for that."

Myra reached behind her and pulled a chair next to the bed. She sat down and scooted close to Didi. "You won't be seeing Jimmy. He was killed in the chase, Didi. He went over the bridge into the water."

Didi's mouth gaped open. Her eyes wide and filled with

horror, she looked from Mitch to Myra. "K-k-killed? No!" she wailed.

"The police have confiscated all the drugs in the apartment, and we have Tootie and Finis in custody. If you want to help yourself, you'd better answer our questions."

Didi's eyes narrowed, and her mouth slowly hardened into a firm line. "I don't know nothin' about no drugs. I never saw any."

Myra chuckled and shook her head. "Now, Didi, you look like a smart girl. You're already facing charges of attempted murder. Don't make it harder on yourself. We might be convinced to ask the district attorney to drop those charges if you can give us information we need about Jimmy."

Didi glared at Myra. "I never seen no drugs."

Myra sighed and stood up. "Okay, have it your way. We tried to help you, but evidently you'd rather spend the better part of your life in jail." She nodded toward the door. "Let's go, Mitch."

They turned and walked toward the door. Just as they pulled the curtain back, Didi called out. "Wait. Come back for a minute."

They stepped back to the bed. "What is it?" Mitch asked.

"You say you can help me if I talk?"

Myra nodded. "Answer our questions truthfully."

Didi sighed and sank back on her pillow. "Okay. What do you wanna know?"

Mitch took out his notepad. "We want to know everything you can tell us about Jimmy's drug organization—the names of everybody working for him, how he gets the drugs into Oxford, and how he launders his money."

Didi closed her eyes for a moment, and a tear left a black mascara mark as it trickled down her cheek. "I don't know the names of all his pushers, but he kept a list. Underneath the cot in the bedroom at that apartment there's some loose boards in the floor. That's where Jimmy hid his laptop with the names of his employees and a running record of what they sold."

Myra smiled at Didi. "Now that's the kind of thing we like to hear. Where did the drugs come from?"

A look of fear crossed Didi's face, and her hand grasped the edge of the bed. "I don't know much about that part. All I know is these guys would come to town every other week, and they'd bring shipments. I think they was from some gang down on the coast, but it scared me just to see 'em. I told Jimmy I didn't wanna be around when they came."

Didi shivered and closed her eyes. Mitch and Myra exchanged glances. For some time the police had suspected that the increase in drug trafficking in Oxford was linked to drug gangs on the Gulf Coast.

"Jimmy had to get rid of all that money some way. How did he launder it?"

Didi opened her eyes and stared at Mitch. "He had different businesses around town running it through their books. I don't know all of 'em, but they're in the computer, too."

Mitch leaned closer to her. "Tell us about Caleb Lawrence. Were you the one who lured him out of Justine's Restaurant the night he was killed?"

Didi's mouth dropped open, and she gasped for breath. "We didn't have nothin' to do with killin' him. Jimmy just wanted to talk to him, that's all. I got him to the alley where Jimmy was, and he roughed Caleb up a little bit."

"Why?"

"'Cause he'd been on that radio show that night, and the chief didn't like it when that guy called in and said Caleb was a friend of Jimmy's."

Mitch felt his heartbeat increase. "Was Caleb a friend of Jimmy's?"

"I wouldn't call him a friend. Jimmy used Caleb's business for laundering money."

Behind him Mitch heard Myra give a little gasp. This development was a complete surprise to them, but Didi had said something else that interested him. "You said the chief sent Jimmy there. Who's that?"

"He's the guy that's head of the ring." Didi laughed. "Jimmy thought he was hot stuff, but he wasn't smart enough to run that big a business. He just did whatever the chief told him."

Mitch felt like he was getting closer to Fala by the moment. He could hardly control his excitement. "Do you know the chief?"

"Yeah." Her eyes grew dark with hatred. "He's a mean one. I'll be glad to see him fall."

"What's his name, Didi?"

Suddenly, Didi began to cough, each one followed by a low moan. Dr. Compton who had stepped into the hall when the questioning began hurried back into the room and bent over her. He checked her monitors before putting the stethoscope to her chest. He turned to Mitch and Myra. "I think you'd better continue this later. She really shouldn't be talking so much."

Mitch nodded, and he and Myra backed toward the door.

Didi reached her uninjured arm out toward them. She struggled to speak.

Mitch stepped back to the bed. "Do you want to tell us the chief's name?"

She coughed and nodded.

"Who is he, Didi?"

She swallowed and struggled to speak. "M-Michael Gr-Grayson."

The news about Michael Grayson had come as a complete surprise to Mitch. No wonder Michael was so eager to get

C.J.'s program off the air. The callers who were concerned about the drug problems in town were getting a little too close to him for comfort.

After they'd left Didi's room, he'd called the station. A few minutes earlier Chief Stoker had contacted him to tell him the laptop had been discovered just where Didi said it was. The technicians had no trouble accessing all the accounts, and arrest warrants were being issued for everyone whose name was recorded there.

Patrol officers were also on the lookout for Michael Grayson and would arrest him when they found him. So far he hadn't shown up at home, and a call to Don Cunningham had revealed that Michael had been fired from WLMT earlier in the day. Mitch wondered what that was about. Maybe C.J. would know.

There were still questions he wanted to ask Didi. So for the time being he and Myra waited for Dr. Compton to let them back in.

Dr. Compton came out of Didi's room and said, "Didi is calm now. She wants to finish talking with you. When you're through, we're going to move her to a room."

"Thanks," Myra said as they headed down the hallway.

Without a word Mitch and Myra reentered Didi's room. Outside Didi's door, Mitch pointed to Myra. "Want to be the good cop?"

She nodded, and they walked inside.

Didi looked surprised as she said, "You're back."

Mitch nodded. "Just a few more questions. Then we'll leave you alone."

"All right."

Mitch took a deep breath. "Tell us what you know about Fala."

A puzzled look came over Didi's face. "Who?"

"Fala. The guy who called in to the radio talk show."

Understanding lit her face, and she shook her head. "We didn't have nothin' to do with Caleb's murder or nobody else."

"Do you deny threatening the talk show host in the parking lot at WLMT?"

Tears formed in her eyes. "We just wanted to scare her. Michael didn't like her talkin' about the drug problem. That was all. We didn't kill nobody."

Mitch stared down at her. "Was Jimmy Carpenter Fala?"

"No," she cried.

Mitch leaned closer. "What about Michael Grayson?"

The look of terror in Didi's eyes reminded Mitch of a trapped animal. "I don't know 'bout him. You'll have to ask him."

"Did you know all the victims had a blond hair in their hands?"

Didi tried to scoot over in the bed to distance herself from Mitch. "No, I didn't know that."

He said, "Your hair's blond. Maybe it was your hair in their hands. Left when you helped murder innocent people."

"No, no," she cried. "I never killed nobody."

Mitch laughed. "I don't believe you. You helped commit those murders. The victims must have pulled some hair from your head when you were stabbing them."

"I swear," Didi cried. "I didn't."

Myra laid a hand on Mitch's arm and pulled him away from the bed. "You're upsetting her, Mitch. There's no need for that." She reached out and caressed Didi's head. "Don't worry. He's just upset. Some of those people were his friends. If you say you didn't do it, I believe you."

Relief shone in Didi's eyes as a tear trickled down the side of her face. "Thank you."

Myra glanced back at Mitch. "I think I know a way we can prove whether or not Didi was involved."

"How?" Didi gasped.

"Let me take one of your hairs," Myra said gently. "We can take it to the lab and have the people there compare it to the ones on the victims. If yours doesn't match those, we'll know you're telling the truth."

Didi nodded and raised her head. "Take all you need. You'll see I'm telling the truth."

Myra reached in her pocket for a plastic envelope, pulled one of Didi's hairs out, and dropped it inside. Sealing it, she returned it to her pocket. "There now. We'll see what the results tell us." She patted Didi's arm. "You get some rest. We'll be back to tell you what the D.A. says about the evidence you've given us. I have a feeling things are going to go real well for you."

"Thank you," Didi said as she smiled at Myra. She turned to Mitch, frowned and rolled over onto her side.

Mitch and Myra walked out of the hospital toward their car. As Mitch guided the car from the parking lot, Myra looked at him. "I think she was telling the truth. What do you think?"

He had asked himself that question the whole time they were in Didi's room. Something still didn't seem right about all this. The murderer had to be Jimmy Carpenter or Michael Grayson. They were the two obvious suspects. Jimmy was dead and Michael would soon be in police custody. Either way, C.J. was safe, and that was the most important thing to him.

"I think she's lying," Mitch said. "She's protecting one of them."

Myra raised her eyebrows before she turned to stare out the windshield. "We'll see."

SIXTEEN

"It's been several hours since Mitch called from the hospital. He said he wasn't hurt, but I keep wondering if he told me that so I wouldn't worry," C.J. said.

Gwen smiled as she studied her friend. "You're different, C.J."

"How?"

"There's a different tone in your voice when you talk about Mitch. I think this time together has been good for the two of you."

Her face grew warm. "Mitch has only been doing his job. Nothing has changed."

The kettle on the stove whistled, distracting her from Gwen's probing gaze, and she busied herself making tea. When she sat down at the table, Gwen picked up her cup and took a sip. As she set it back in the saucer, a little smile pulled at her mouth. "Are you sure nothing has changed?"

C.J. paused, and thought for a moment. The expectant look on Gwen's face said she demanded an answer. C.J. opened her mouth to respond, but stopped at the sound of the front doorbell. She pushed her chair back, sprang to her feet and dashed toward the entry.

When she opened the door, Mitch stepped inside. His

shoulders slumped, and his eyes looked weary, as they had so many times in the past when he'd been working on a difficult case. She wished she could tell him how glad she was to see him, but fear of rejection kept her quiet.

He smiled at her and stepped forward. "It's been a long day."

She motioned toward the kitchen. "Gwen and I are having a cup of tea. Come have one with us and tell us everything that's happened."

He stared at her for a moment, then nodded and took off his coat. "Okay."

She walked back to the kitchen with him right behind. Gwen jumped up and gave him a quick hug as he came through the door. "You look exhausted, Mitch."

A pang of regret stabbed C.J. How easy it was for Gwen to express her concern for Mitch. What made her hold back, when all she wanted was to wrap her arms around him and never let him go? She turned away and reached for a cup. Otto barked in the backyard, but Mitch didn't seem to hear it.

"It's been a hard day," he said. "It's been a while since I went on a drug raid, but I have to admit I got an adrenaline rush when it all started. Dean has a dangerous job."

For the next few minutes he related the events of the day, ending with the interrogation of Didi in the hospital. "But the biggest surprise of all came when she revealed that Jimmy wasn't the head of the drug ring."

C.J. and Gwen gaped at each other. "Then who was?" C.J. demanded.

Mitch glanced from one to the other. "Hang on to your hats, girls. You're not going to believe this."

Gwen looked like she was ready to burst. "Who?"

He paused a moment as if for dramatic effect before he spoke. "Michael Grayson."

"What?" They screamed in unison.

"None other than the head of advertising at your station," Mitch said.

C.J. sank back in her chair in stunned silence. "It all makes sense now. That's why he wanted us off the air. We were generating too many calls about drugs in Oxford, and he didn't like the notoriety."

Gwen jumped up and pounded the table. "That worm! I can hardly wait for Mr. Cunningham to hear about this."

C.J. sprang up beside her and grabbed her hand. "Oh, Gwen, I wish we could tell Harley. Can you imagine how he would have played it up? When this hits the news, there's no telling how many calls we'll get on the show."

Mitch stood up, a frown pulling at his eyebrows. "Whoa, back up. What show? I thought you were off the air."

C.J. laughed. "Not anymore. We've had quite a day, too."

Mitch listened as she told him what had transpired at the radio station and about Mr. Cunningham's call to them. "So we're back on beginning next Monday, and Gwen has been promoted to producer."

Mitch's dark-eyed stare bored into C.J. "No, you can't do this. Not yet."

"Why not?"

"We're still not sure about Fala. I don't want you back on the radio until we know the case is solved."

C.J. frowned. "But you said you believed that either Jimmy Carpenter or Michael Grayson was Fala."

The muscle in his jaw twitched, and he leaned forward. "We don't know that for sure. You're not going back on until we're positive."

The commanding tone of his voice set her teeth on edge, and her defenses rose. C.J. clenched her fist and glared at him. "You can't tell me what to do."

Glaring right back, he said, "For once in your life would you forget your stubbornness and listen to me?"

Gwen held up her hands and backed away. "Hey, guys, I think I'll go in the den until you sort this out."

C.J. watched her go and then turned back to Mitch. Her body quivered with anger. "You know one of them had to be Fala. You've never wanted me on that show, and you're just using this as an excuse to keep me from doing what I want."

A bewildered expression crossed his face before he straightened and raked his hand through his hair. "Why do you always do this? You defy me on everything I try to do to help you."

"Help me? You're trying to ease me right out of my job."

He sighed. "I'm not. I just want you to be safe." He reached toward her, but she backed away. "Give Myra and me some time to get to the bottom of this. When we know Fala's caught, you can go back on the air."

The mention of Myra infuriated her further. "If you aren't sure who Fala is, then you shouldn't be standing here wasting time. You need to get with that partner of yours and determine whether or not you've found the killer."

His face drained of color, and he stared at her. "Maybe it's been wrong of me to stay so close to you during this investigation. I did it because I wanted to protect you and because I still love you. But suddenly it's clear to me there's no future for us. We have nothing in common."

This was different than anything he'd said to her before. Her heart skipped a beat at the defeat she could see in his face. "Wh-what do you mean?"

He moved away from her. "I'm a believer, and you're not. There's no way we can ever come together with that problem between us. I know now I can't have a wife who doesn't share my beliefs. You refuse to accept God's love, and you've turned your back on me. I love you, but I can't do this anymore. I'm going back to the station to file my report. I'll have one of the other officers take my place until this case is closed."

She wanted to throw her arms around him and beg him to stay. Anger mingled with dread at the thought of his not being with her, but maybe he was right. She couldn't accept the idea of depending on some unseen God. She squared her shoulders. "That's fine with me."

He stood still for a moment, then turned and hurried from the room. She waited until the front door slammed before she sank down at the table and buried her face in her hands.

A thought, almost like a small voice, gnawed at the back of her mind—one she'd ignored for a long time. Its whispers told her of the way to peace, but she pushed it away. She'd trusted it when she was a child, but it hadn't helped her mother.

She'd prayed and begged her mother to take her and leave, but drugs can destroy the ability to reason. C.J. knew her mother loved her, but the chase for the next fix had consumed the mind and body of the beautiful woman her mother had been. Sometimes her mother didn't seem to mind the beatings as long as there was the reward of drug euphoria at the end.

She'd prayed for her father, also. Those prayers hadn't stopped him from being drunk and high on drugs the night he'd crashed his car into a tree.

C.J. had hoped things would change after his death, but they hadn't. Nothing changed until the day her mother deserted her in a mall in Nashville. After that it was one foster home after another, and God was never mentioned in those places.

Perhaps she should have told Mitch all the things that had happened to her, but those painful memories needed to be ignored. To think about them only caused her anguish. Now they had helped to drive Mitch away, and she didn't know if she could recover from that.

Tears blinding her, she jumped up from the table and ran

from the kitchen to her bedroom. Throwing herself on the bed, she buried her face in a pillow and pulled it tight.

Sobs shook her body. "Help me," she moaned.

The small voice niggled again, its whisper so familiar. She reached out to draw the sound nearer, but it welled up from inside her. Although she'd ignored its plea for years, the time had come when she had to admit the truth—it was the presence of God.

Mitch strode from the front porch to his car. Jerking the door open, he climbed inside and gazed in anger at C.J.'s house.

Confusion flooded through him. What had happened in there? One minute they were discussing the arrests of the day, and the next C.J. was accusing him of trying to control her.

He leaned forward, his head resting on the steering wheel, and closed his eyes. The events of the day were catching up with him, and his body screamed with weariness. Sleep—that's what he needed. Eight hours of uninterrupted unconsciousness.

For a moment he considered going back to his apartment. Forget about reports and protecting C.J. It was time he looked out for himself. Paperwork could be done tomorrow, and C.J. could take care of herself from now on. With a frown he twisted the key in the ignition and put the car in Reverse. At the end of the driveway, he braked and glanced back at the house.

Mitch wondered if she really understood that he wouldn't be coming back. He pulled his cell phone from the clip on his belt and flipped it open. It was easier to tell her over the phone.

His finger punched the first number and paused. He was still a policeman. With a sigh he tossed the cell phone on the seat beside him and backed into the street. Just a few more days, and he wouldn't need to see her anymore.

Then he could get on with his life.

* * *

C.J. sat up on the side of the bed. Guilt pricked her conscience. Gwen must think she'd been abandoned. C.J. studied her reflection in the mirror before she headed for the door. One look at her red eyes and Gwen would know the reason for her absence.

Gwen sat at the kitchen table, Otto in her lap, when C.J. entered. "I talked to Adam while you were in the bedroom, and he had some good news. I told him about Jimmy and Michael." A stricken look crossed her face, and she pursed her lips. "It was okay to tell him, wasn't it?"

"I suppose so. With the drug raid and the warrant for Michael's arrest, it's all a matter of public record now."

Gwen crooked her index finger and pretended to wipe it across her brow. "Whew! I thought maybe I'd revealed some classified police information or something."

C.J. couldn't help but laugh. Gwen had the gift of cheering her up like no one else she'd ever known. "So, what's the news?"

"Oh, yeah. Adam finished his painting, so he wants to cook dinner for us. I told him we'd be over when you finished resting."

"That sounds good. What time are we due there?"

"I told him we could come anytime to help him cook."

C.J. smiled at the way Gwen's eyes lit up when she talked about Adam. It reminded her of how she'd felt when she knew she was falling in love with Mitch. "Why don't you go on over, and I'll come in a little while. I have some ideas for the show I want to get down on paper while they're on my mind."

Gwen frowned. "Are you sure that's a good idea? I don't want to leave you alone."

Otto growled, and they both looked down at him. C.J. dropped to her knees and hugged the little dog. "I think he's trying to tell you I'm well protected. Besides, you're going to be right across the street. I'll be there soon."

Gwen's brow wrinkled. "Well, if you're sure."

"Go on. Help Adam cook. Enjoy your time together before I get there."

Gwen grinned. "Since you put it that way, I'll go. Please don't take too long."

"I won't," C.J. promised. "Now go, and lock the front door on your way out."

Gwen gave a little salute and ran toward the front of the house. "Will do. See you soon."

C.J. stood in the kitchen, smiling to herself until she heard the click of the front door. She was so glad Gwen and Adam were interested in each other. They both deserved happiness, and she hoped they could find it together.

Shaking her head, C.J. headed into the den and sat down at her computer. As the computer booted, she realized she hadn't checked her e-mail all day. She opened the in-box and scanned down the list of waiting messages.

"No!" Fala's sender name stood out in bold print. She reached for the mouse and clicked.

One more chance for this sad game,
You haven't guessed, that's quite a shame.
Three that blinked and now there's one
Who'll be next to have some fun?
Fala

SEVENTEEN

Her eyes grew wide. She was alone, and Fala was alive. She had to get out of the house. Adam and Gwen were expecting her. *Run there,* her mind screamed.

With Otto barking at her heels, she ran to her bedroom. She grabbed her jacket from the closet and hurried back toward the door.

Otto. She had to take care of him before she left. His crate sat in the corner of her bedroom. She scooped him up and deposited him inside. "Be a good boy until I get back. I won't be gone long."

The key ring with the attached small pepper spray canister lay on her dresser next to her cell phone. She picked it up, dropped it in her pants pocket and turned to leave, but she paused at another thought.

Mitch needed to know Fala was alive. She picked up her cell phone and dialed. A frown creased her brow when his voice mail answered. That wasn't like him. He always kept his phone on. Maybe he saw her number on caller ID and didn't want to talk to her.

When the voice mail beeped, she took a deep breath. "Mitch, this is C.J. I wanted you to know I received another e-mail from Fala. He's promised another murder. Call me when you get this message. I'm on my way to Adam's house for dinner." A strangled cry ripped from her throat. "Oh, Mitch. Please call me."

She flipped the phone closed and dropped it in her jacket pocket. Without a backward glance she ran from the house and toward the welcoming lights shining in Adam's windows. Just a few steps, and she'd be safe with Adam and Gwen.

The squad room of the police station appeared deserted as Mitch walked in. He headed straight for his office, his pending report on his mind.

Jennie, the day dispatcher, almost collided with him as she walked out the door of his office just as he arrived there. He grabbed her arm to keep her from falling. "Sorry, Jennie, I didn't see you. What are you doing here so late?"

She straightened up and smiled. "Working some overtime, but I'm leaving now. I left a message from Bill Diamond on your desk. He called and said he'd been trying to reach you on your cell phone, but you weren't answering."

"I didn't hear…" Mitch stopped in surprise as his hand touched the empty clip on his belt. He frowned, trying to think where he'd left his phone, then he remembered. "Oh, I put it in the seat of the car. It must still be there."

Jennie eased around him. "Well, anyway, he said to give him a call." She headed down the hall. "Gotta run. See you tomorrow."

Mitch watched her go before he went in and settled behind his desk. Excitement filled him as he read the note in front of him. He dialed the number. His fingers drummed on the desk as he waited for an answer.

"Bill Diamond."

Mitch sat up straight. "Bill, Mitch Harmon. Sorry I missed you. Do you have anything for me?"

Bill chuckled. "Do I ever. I think you're going to like this."

Mitch reached for his notebook and a pen. "What did you find out?"

Papers shuffled in the background on the other end of the line. "I printed out all this stuff they sent from Quantico, but I'll e-mail it to you so you can look over it, too." More shuffling sounded before he spoke again. "There, now, I think I have it all in order. Ready?"

Every nerve in his body tingled. "Ready."

"Okay, here's what I have. Your crimes fit the M.O. of a serial killer the FBI has been tracking across the country. They don't know for sure how many times he's struck, but there are several similar reported cases. The killer is believed to be a guy named Jack Horn, but he's been dubbed the Acronym Killer."

Mitch scribbled furiously. "Acronym Killer? Why?"

"I think you'll understand when I tell you about this guy. He's a half-blooded Crow Indian."

Mitch's pen almost slipped from his fingers. "Did you say *Crow?*"

"Yeah. Why?"

"Because I found out the name *Fala* meant a crow, but I thought it referred to a bird, not the Native American tribe."

Bill chuckled. "Yeah, sometimes our investigations can take us in the wrong direction. Anyway, Jack's mother was Crow and his father was a cowboy who disappeared before he was born. He and his mother lived on the reservation in Montana until she died when he was about ten. He watched her being raped and murdered by a bunch of drunken cowboys from a nearby ranch. After that he was taken in by an old lady in town who had a soft spot for orphans."

"Is she still living?"

"Nope. She raised and educated him, but died while he was

in college. He came back just long enough to liquidate all her holdings, which she'd left to him. Before he left town, though, there were four murders. After he disappeared, the local sheriff put all the pieces together when a painting arrived at his office."

Mitch glanced up from writing and frowned. "What was it?

"A picture of Two Rivers High School. Jack graduated from there, and he had trouble being bullied by some of his classmates—some guys named James Townsend, Paul Rutherford and Matthew Hatton. It seemed they were encouraged by a coach named Thomas Scofield. Jack complained that they picked on him, but nobody would do anything about it. All four were stabbed to death, beginning with Townsend. Then the sheriff received the painting and figured out it was Jack who killed them."

"How?"

"Each victim's last name started with a letter in the school's initials—TRHS—Townsend, Rutherford, Hatton, and Scofield. The fact that Jack was a good artist and everybody in town knew he held a grudge against the four of them nailed it for him."

Mitch gave a low whistle. "I see." A thought popped into his head. "What about the crime scenes?"

"At the first one, there were bloody handprints everywhere, at the second a gun was taken, at the third a truck was stolen and at the fourth they found a letter taking credit for leading a great war party."

"Whoa, there," Mitch interrupted. "You lost me on the fourth one. We haven't had a fourth murder yet."

"I know. The fourth one is when Jack leaves a note detailing how his murder spree has paralleled the tests that young Crow boys had to pass to become a warrior."

"But that's crazy," Mitch said. "What do these murders have to do with that?"

Bill sighed. "I guess in his twisted mind it's the same thing. When the Crow nation was strong, a boy only achieved manhood and became a warrior after proving himself in battle. He had to have proof that he touched his enemies. That's why he leaves handprints. He also had to steal a weapon and a horse from his enemies, and then he had to recount many deaths."

Scenes from the murders flashed through Mitch's head. "That explains the handprints at Mary's, the missing knife from Caleb and the truck stolen from Harley."

"I hope you can stop him before there's a fourth."

Mitch's stomach roiled. "So do I. If I only knew where to look." Mitch picked up the pen again. "Tell me where else the Acronym Killer struck."

"Ummm, let's see." Papers shuffled again. "The first was in Montana, the second was in Florida at the South Beach Retirement Center—SBRC. Victims were Anne Simpson, Maxwell Barron, Timothy Ross and Director Ed Crawford. The next one was in Ohio at the New Prospect General Hospital—NPGH. Victims were Gina Noland, Jimmy Perry, Hazel Gross and Administrator Larry Hammonds. Each time a painting of the building with its logo on it arrived after the murders."

Mitch swallowed back the fear he felt welling up in him. He knew the importance of keeping an open mind until all the evidence was in, but this information was sending goose bumps all over his body. "Do you have a picture of Jack in the file?"

"Yeah, it's from his high school yearbook. It should give you an idea of who you're looking for."

"Thanks, Bill. I appreciate your help on this case. If I can ever do anything for you, let me know."

"You're welcome, Mitch. Remember, this is an open investigation with the bureau. If you find out anything about this guy, get in touch with me. I'm going to e-mail this file to you. You should have it in a few minutes."

Mitch hung up and paced across the room. A serial killer was different from any other murderer he'd dealt with before. He thought of Jimmy Carpenter and Michael Grayson. Neither one looked as if he could have a Native American heritage, but Bill had said Jack Horn's father was a white man.

The computer chimed the arrival of an e-mail, and Mitch hurried to it. Bill's sender name popped up beside the message. With shaking fingers he opened the attached file and scrolled through it. The report appeared very thorough, and he caught glimpses of things Bill had told him—Two Rivers High School, New Prospect General Hospital.

He scrolled on past, looking for the picture. It rolled into view, and he leaned forward to study the face on the screen. His body began to shake. His arm hit some papers lying on the desk, and they went flying in all different directions. He stared at the picture before him, his head slowly shaking back and forth.

"It can't be," he whispered.

Mitch's fist struck his desk as he stared at the young face of Adam Connor on his computer screen. How could he have been so blind?

Blood pounded in his ears as he grabbed for the telephone. C.J.! He had to tell her. Adam lived right across the street from her house. He dialed C.J.'s home phone, and after several rings, he heard her voice. "I'm sorry. I can't come to the phone right now. Leave a message."

Where could she be? She and Gwen weren't supposed to leave the house. "C.J.," he yelled after the beep, "Don't go near Adam! He's Fala! I'm on my way."

He disconnected the call and dialed her cell phone. When it went to voice mail, he repeated the message, his voice growing louder with each word.

Panic overtook him, and he rushed from his office to the dispatch area. "Alert patrol officers that Adam Connor is Fala.

He's wanted by the FBI," he yelled at Chet, the night dispatcher. "He lives at 410 Lansdowne Drive. Get somebody over there right away. I'll meet them there."

He ran from the building and jumped in his car. His cell phone with the voice mail blinking lay on the seat beside him. He scooped up the phone and listened to his messages. Within seconds, he heard Bill Diamond's message, deleted it and listened to the next one. Relief at hearing C.J.'s voice quickly turned to fear as she told him she was going to Adam's for dinner. "No," he cried.

The message had been left over an hour ago. Why had he left his phone in the car when he stopped at that diner on the way to the station? His heart pounded with fear at the thought of C.J. with Adam. He had to warn her.

His fingers shook so violently that he could hardly put in Adam's number. When his answering machine picked up, Mitch groaned. Where could they be? Only one option seemed to present itself at the moment. He slammed on the accelerator and sped out of the parking lot. He had to get to Adam's house right away. He needed to save C.J.

EIGHTEEN

Gwen smiled at C.J. from across the table. "Would you like more coffee?"

C.J. held her hand over the top of her cup. "None for me."

She settled back and gazed around Adam's dining room. It was so peaceful here. She wished that she could close her eyes and forget what she discovered before she ran across the street to the safety of Adam's house.

"You're a million miles away, C.J.," Adam's voice broke into her thoughts.

The sound startled her, and she straightened in her chair. "I was just thinking how nice it is here. It's good to be with friends so I can try to forget that Fala is out there waiting to take another life."

"Don't think about that now. Maybe Mitch will have some news," Gwen said.

C.J. gave a little grunt. "Yeah, if I ever see him again."

Adam frowned and stared at her. "Of course you'll see him again. I'll bet he comes by tonight."

Tears formed in her eyes. "I don't know. I left a message for him, and he hasn't called me yet."

Gwen reached across the table and grasped C.J.'s hand. "Have you checked your cell phone since you've been here?"

C.J. glanced toward the living room. "No, it's in my jacket, and I hung it on the hall tree when I came in."

Adam jumped up. "I'll get it for you, and you can see if you missed him."

He hurried from the room and returned in a few moments. C.J. took the phone from him, flipped it open, then tossed it onto the table. "Nothing."

Adam said, "Maybe he called you at home. Tell you what, I'll wash the dishes, and then we can go to your house and check your answering machine. I'll bet there's a message waiting."

The thought bolstered her spirits. "That sounds good, but let me help."

Adam held up a hand. "No, you're our guest of honor tonight. Just relax, and Gwen and I will clean up the kitchen."

C.J. started to protest, but changed her mind. "Okay, I'll just make a trip to the bathroom and then join you."

Adam and Gwen gathered up the last dishes and headed toward the kitchen. He inclined his head in the direction of the hallway that led to the back of the house. "You know where the bathroom is. Make yourself at home. We won't be but a minute."

She'd been in Adam's home many times, and the layout was very much like hers, as were so many of the homes in their subdivision. Her home had three bedrooms, but she knew Adam had converted the bedroom on the right side of the hall to his studio. As she passed by it, she noticed the door was cracked open a little. A soft light glowed within.

She glanced around to see if Adam or Gwen had followed her, but she could hear voices coming from the kitchen. Reaching out, she pushed on the door. With a slight creak it swung open. Paintings hung on the walls, and other canvases sat propped against each other all around the room.

An easel, a spotlight from the ceiling illuminating it, sat in the center of the room. Something about the painting resting on it drew her into the room. Her heart pounded in awe at the brilliant colors sprawled across the canvas.

She'd attended a showing of abstract art once when she was in college, and the work before her reminded her of some she'd seen. But there was something different about this one. Trying to determine what Adam had intended to convey, she tilted her head to one side and stared at the vivid splashes. Then she saw it—barely visible underneath the sweeps of color—the radio station with its lit call letters standing atop the building. The WLMT sign blinked in the darkness.

Confusion filled her. Why would Adam paint the station? The light from overhead shimmered on the sign, making its beams glow even brighter in the painting.

"WLMT," she whispered. "WLMT."

From deep in the recesses of her mind, a thought forced its way to the surface. Her eyes widened in horror. East to west, stand tall, giant flames, three that blinked—clues from the riddles that led to the WLMT sign. The letters of the sign held the answer. But what?

She pressed her hand to her head. WLMT. What could the sign have to do with the three murders? Her mind raced. Mary, Caleb, and Harley. No, that didn't make sense.

Suddenly, she shivered. Warren, Lawrence, and Martin— their last names matched the call letters. But who was the *T?*

She clamped her hand over her mouth to keep from screaming. *T* for Tanner. She was the next intended victim! She whirled around to run, but staggered backward in surprise at the sight before her.

Adam stood in the door, Gwen in front of him. His left arm encircled her waist, and his right hand held Gwen's gun to her head. Gwen's fear-filled eyes stared at C.J. like an animal caught in an inescapable snare.

A shrill laugh pierced the room, Fala's voice, but it was coming from Adam's mouth. "Found my little masterpiece, did you?"

Terror propelled her backward into the easel, and the painting tumbled to the floor. "Adam, what are you doing?"

He laughed again. "Finishing the game, C.J. I told you to solve the riddles, but you didn't. And now you're too late."

Gwen's face turned white, and she gagged as if she were about to throw up. "Adam, let Gwen go," C.J. pleaded.

"Not on your life." He stood silent for a moment, and then broke into hysterical laughter. When he calmed down, he shook his head. "I made a joke. Not on your life. Get it? And that's exactly what it's come down to, C.J.—your life."

She shook her head in bewilderment. "I don't understand. I thought you were my friend. Why would you want to hurt me?"

He lifted an eyebrow and gazed at her. "It's nothing personal. I like you. A lot. But you just happen to be the next one to fall in the game." His tongue clucked at her. "Shame on you for not figuring out the riddles. Now it's over."

Panic filled her. "What are you going to do?"

He pulled Gwen's face next to his and nuzzled her cheek with his. "Why, kill both of you." He straightened up. "But not here in my house. I think we'll take a ride to the radio station in Gwen's car. I put the keys in it while Gwen was helping me cook dinner. You drive, and Gwen and I will sit in the backseat. One wrong move, and your friend dies instantly. Understand?"

C.J. swallowed. "I understand."

Adam backed into the hallway and motioned with his head for C.J. to move in front of him. They walked back through the house. Their footsteps pealed like a death knell in C.J.'s ears. She scanned the dining table as they passed, but her cell phone no longer lay there.

As if reading her thoughts, Adam spoke. "It's gone, C.J. You won't need a cell phone any longer."

She moved to the front door and reached for her jacket on the hall tree, but Adam's voice stopped her. "You don't need that, either. All you have to do right now is drive."

C.J. stepped into the cold night air and shivered. She glanced up at the stars twinkling in the clear sky. The heavens were aglow tonight, and she thought she'd never seen a more beautiful sight. She stopped and gazed upward, relishing the scene she'd taken for granted so many times before. It all held a different meaning on this night.

"Get in the car," Adam ordered.

She moved to Gwen's Toyota and climbed into the front seat. Behind her Adam and Gwen crawled in. A whimper cut through the silence, and C.J. wanted to turn and reassure her friend. But she had no reason to believe this was going to turn out any differently than Adam had said.

She turned on the ignition, backed into the street and began the drive to the radio station. There had to be some way out of their predicament, but she couldn't think over the pounding of her heart. She took one hand off the steering wheel and rubbed the side of her head. Where could she find some help?

Suddenly, the voice that had pulled at her thoughts for days returned. It whispered words of peace. If she were to save the two of them, she had to remain calm. She took a deep breath and relaxed. Her tight grip on the steering wheel eased, and her shoulders rested against the back of the seat.

She glanced in the rearview mirror and caught a glimpse of Adam's face as they passed a streetlight. His crazed eyes were not those of the man she'd known as her friend. They were those of a maniacal killer, bent on completing the deadly game he'd begun with her weeks before. She was just now beginning to understand the rules and what was at stake, and she was ready to play.

She cleared her throat. "Adam, if you wanted to kill me, why did three other people have to die?"

He laughed. "Because those are the rules. There are four tasks to complete before becoming a warrior."

C.J. sat up a little straighter. "What kind of warrior?"

Adam leaned forward, pulling Gwen with him. "You wouldn't understand, C.J. It's part of my heritage."

"But why Mary? She was so kind to you."

In the rearview mirror she saw him shrug. "Her last name happened to start with the right letter."

C.J. frowned. "One thing I don't understand, though, is how you got into and out of Mary's house. The doors were all locked."

A shrill laugh came from the backseat. "You played right into my hands on that one. I was so glad to help you out with errands like taking your car to get the tires changed. Remember that?"

"But that was weeks ago. I gave you the keys to my car, and you brought it back after the garage had gotten the new tires on."

"Yes, and it just so happened that the key to Mary's house was on that ring. It was so simple. Get a duplicate made, and then slip into her house while she was sleeping. Otto was so glad to see the treat I brought him that he didn't even bark."

The thought of Adam sneaking into Mary's house caused her to shiver. "And Caleb? Why him?"

"That took a little work. I had to keep suggesting to Gwen that he'd make a good guest for your show before she took the hint." A smacking sound came from the backseat, and C.J. knew Adam had kissed Gwen on the cheek.

"Don't touch me!" Gwen cried.

Adam chuckled. "You weren't saying that a little while ago. You were throwing yourself at me like you'd never had a man's attention before."

C.J. stole a glance over her shoulder. "And you killed Harley."

"Yeah." He giggled like a child. "It was really very funny. He drove into the garage and got out of his truck. He didn't see me at first. Then when he heard me, he got all scared and said, 'Is somebody there?'"

C.J. fought back the tears filling her eyes. "We don't want to hear this."

"He backed up against the door of the truck and tried to peer into the darkness." Adam continued as if he hadn't heard her. "When I stepped out of the shadows, he tensed and then relaxed with recognition. 'What are you doing here?' he said."

"Please, Adam," Gwen moaned.

He laughed again. "I stepped up to him and plunged the knife in before he knew what was happening. You should have seen the shock on his face. When I stabbed him the second time, I said, 'C.J. sends her best.'"

If C.J. lived through the night, there would be time later to mourn for Mary, Caleb and Harley, but now she had other, more pressing concerns. Ahead, the radio station came into view. Tonight three of the letters blinked on top of the building. A chill of doom surged through her at the sight of the *T* standing dark against the night sky. She parked in the space next to the door and sat still. "Now what?"

"We get out and go inside. Gwen and I will follow you, C.J."

Her fingers curled around the door handle, and she turned slightly so she could see Adam. "You've already killed three people, and I'm slated to be your fourth victim. You don't need Gwen. Let her go, and she won't tell anyone your identity."

Adam shook his head in disgust. "C.J., you disappoint me. Gwen would run right to the police. But you're right. There are usually only four victims, but this time I'm making an exception. You see, there was some evidence at each of the crime scenes. Do you know what it was?"

"A blond hair in each one's hand," Gwen whispered.

Adam gave her another kiss on the cheek. "That's right, darling, and they belonged to you. I helped myself to some hairs from your brush when I had dinner at your house. Now after I kill C.J., you're going to be the victim of an apparent suicide, shot with your own gun. The note by your body will confess that you are Fala and that you couldn't live with yourself after killing four people."

C.J.'s eyes grew wide. "Adam, you're not only crazy, you're evil."

He smiled. "And smart." He gestured toward the building. "Now bring the car keys and let's go to Gwen's office."

C.J. unlocked the front door of the building with Gwen's key and led the way into the dark radio station. Hoping Adam wouldn't notice that she didn't relock the door, she pulled out the key and stepped into the building. "Do you want me to turn on the lights?"

"No." Adam guided Gwen through the door.

A little cry escaped Gwen's mouth as she stumbled forward, the gun still pointed at her head. Her knees bent, and her body sagged forward. C.J. reached out to catch her, but Adam jerked Gwen back upright. His hand snaked through her hair and pulled her head backward as the gun rubbed her temple.

C.J. clenched her fists. "Quit tormenting her."

"It's just begun, C.J. I have so much more planned for you two tonight." He laughed and motioned for C.J. to proceed up the stairs.

She hurried to the steps and climbed to the second floor, to Gwen's office. Once inside, C.J. turned to him. "What now, Adam?"

He pulled a flashlight from his pocket and shone it on the closet across the room. "There's a key to that closet on Gwen's key ring. I want you to lock her in there for the time being."

Gwen began to cry. "Please, Adam, no."

"Shut up!" He shoved her across the room. She fell on the floor and hit her head against the closet door.

C.J. ran and knelt beside her. "Stay calm," she whispered in Gwen's ear. "I'm going to lock you in the closet as he said. I don't know how, but I know we're going to live through this."

Gwen bit her trembling lip as they pushed to their feet. The beam from the flashlight illuminated her tear-stained face. She grabbed C.J. and hugged her. "I'm praying, C.J. God be with you."

The words flowed over C.J., and in that moment she knew where the voice in her head came from. She might have tried to forget God, but He had never left her side. She closed her eyes and felt His presence flow through her.

So this was what Mitch had been trying to tell her. A peace like she'd never known welled up in her, and she welcomed it. She closed her eyes and smiled. "God is with us both."

"What's all the whispering about?" Adam yelled. "Get her in that closet now."

C.J. grasped her friend's hand, opened the door, and Gwen stepped inside. C.J. turned the key in the lock and slowly faced Adam. "Now what?"

"Now we go to the roof. I think it's almost poetic that you're going to die by the sign. Since you didn't figure out the riddle, the last thing you'll see will be those letters reminding you of the game you lost."

Adam stood beside Gwen's desk, and C.J. eased across the room toward him. "You're not going to get away with this. Mitch will hunt you down. He won't let a crazy killer like you go free."

"You think so? No one's touched me yet, and Mitch won't, either."

C.J. stepped closer, her hand outstretched. "Don't underestimate him. He'll be here any moment."

Adam laughed. "Now who's the crazy one? He has no idea where you are. Remember? He didn't answer the phone."

Her arm swung beside her body as she neared him. "Any minute now, he'll rush in." She stopped and cocked an ear. "What's that?"

Adam glanced over his shoulder. "What?"

"This!"

She reached out and grabbed the small lamp sitting on the side of Gwen's desk. With one quick sweep, her arm swung the lamp, hitting Adam on the side of the head. He reeled backward, stumbling to keep from falling. C.J. advanced and struck at him again. His legs gave way, and he fell to the floor.

The lamp dropped from her hand, and C.J. ran into the hallway. Adam's voice rang out from the office. "You don't fool me. You won't run and leave your friend here."

His words brought her up short, and she looked around, desperate to find a hiding place. A crashing sound, like a chair being turned over, came from Gwen's office. Adam was getting to his feet. She willed her trembling legs to run, and she sped down the hall toward the broadcast booths.

Behind her Adam's voice roared. "Ready or not, here I come."

She had to find a place to hide and deal with the fact that Fala had been one of her most trusted friends. If she could just think, she might come up with a way she could escape. Failure to elude him meant she and Gwen would surely die. At that moment she didn't know how she would do it, but she had to stop Adam.

NINETEEN

C.J. raced down the long second-floor hallway of the radio station toward Mr. Cunningham's office. Adam would have to look in the other rooms before he got there. Ducking inside, she grabbed the phone and dropped to her knees. She wedged her body inside the opening between the desk's two pedestals and dialed.

A voice answered within seconds. "9-1-1. What is your emergency?"

"This is C. J. Tanner. I'm at WLMT radio station. Adam Connor is trying to kill Gwen Anderson and me. He's the guy named Fala that the police are looking for. I need help right away."

"I'll have officers there in a few minutes. Where are you now?"

"I'm in an office on the second floor, hiding. He has Gwen locked in a closet in her office."

"Where is the man now?"

"He's searching for me. He has a gun."

"Can you stay hidden until the officers get there?"

"I don't…"

"C.J.," Adam's voice cried, "where are you?"

His footsteps echoed in the hallway. Her hand froze on the

phone. "He's going to find me. How long will it be before the officers are here?"

"They're on the way. It won't be much longer."

A thought struck her all of a sudden. "Get word to Mitch Harmon. Tell him Adam is Fala."

"We will. Just stay calm."

A door banged against the wall from the direction of the broadcast booth. "All right, C.J.," Adam snarled. "I'm tired of this. If you don't come out in one minute, I'm going back to Gwen's office to kill her. It really doesn't matter which order you die in."

"He's going to kill my friend," she whispered into the phone. "I can't stay here."

"Don't expose yourself!" the voice on the line said.

"Tell the officers the front door of the station is unlocked. I have to go."

"Stay in your hiding place," the voice begged.

"C.J.!" Adam roared.

Another door rattled. C.J. placed the phone on the floor and crawled out from under the desk. She crept to the door and listened for movement. Adam was getting closer to her hiding place every moment. A weapon—that's what she needed.

As she slid back against the wall, her head struck something hard. A wooden plaque with an engraved gold plate attached hung behind her—an award of some kind. She pulled it from the wall and held it above her head.

In the hallway Adam's slow steps approached the office. "You've gotta be in here, C.J. Make it easier on yourself and come out now."

Her breath stopped as he paused outside the door. She slunk farther into the shadows. The doorknob rotated, and the door inched forward, opening away from her. She could see

Adam's hand pushing it wider. "Come out, C.J. Don't make me come after you."

Her fingers holding the plaque trembled, and she gripped it harder. The barrel of the gun appeared, and then he stepped into the room.

One more step. Take one more step.

He eased across the threshold and toward the desk. In a flash she bolted forward and brought the plaque down on his head with the full force of her weight. He stumbled forward, and she advanced, hitting him again.

He staggered sideways. C.J. ran from the office and through the hallway toward the staircase. Lead him away from Gwen, she kept thinking. Run. Give the police time to get here.

A roar of rage echoed through the quiet. Running footsteps pursued her, and she charged on until she reached the stairs and began to descend. Halfway down, she caught sight of the streetlight outside shining through the glass of the front door. She fixed her eyes on that target and fled faster.

Suddenly, her foot slipped on the second step from the bottom. Her body fell forward, and she clutched at the railing. She clawed at empty air as she flew through space and landed in a heap, her head striking the hard entry hall floor.

Before she could get to her feet, a strong hand clamped around her arm, and the cold steel of a gun pressed against her temple. "You're gonna pay for that, C.J.," Adam's voice growled in her ear.

With one hand, he jerked her to her feet and clamped his arm around her waist, the gun still pressed against her head. She struggled to move, but he held her tight. He placed his cheek next to hers and growled in her ear. "It's no use," he said. "You can't escape."

A sticky, wet substance trickled from his head, and she could feel its dampness on her cheek. Blood. The thought

made her retch, and she struggled to control the spasms wash-
ing over her.

He turned her around and forced her toward the stairs.
Although she strained to hear, there was no sound of sirens
in the night. Stall. Give them time to get here. "What are you
going to do?" she asked.

His lips pressed against her ear. "Now we're going to the
roof." He pushed her forward, and she stumbled on the first
step. He jerked her upright and snarled. "No more moves, C.J.
This game is over." He pulled her tighter against him. "Check-
mate," he whispered.

Mitch gripped the steering wheel as the car sped through
the streets. The message on his phone had been left at least
two hours ago. He might already be too late.

The streetlights blurred in his vision as he raced down
the street. His heart pounded out a staccato tattoo in his
ears. He cast his eyes upwards. Stars dotted the sky like
twinkling diamonds.

His hands relaxed on the steering wheel, and he breathed
deeply. For weeks he'd been trying to determine Fala's identity,
and now that he knew, he had no idea which way to turn.

Adam wasn't at home. Why was he going there? There was
no way he could figure this out on his own, but he knew where
to turn. "God, help me. Show me what to do. Don't let her die."

He slowed the car. There was something he was missing,
and he struggled to think what it was. Up ahead he spied an
all-night convenience store, and he made a high-speed U-turn
in the parking lot. The car, now headed in the opposite direction, raced back into the street.

Why he turned around, he didn't know, but he was positive
he'd been going the wrong way. "I don't know what to do,
God. Help me."

He had to think. Remember what the FBI file said. There'd been paintings. What about them?

Bill Diamond's words flashed into his mind: *Each time a painting of the building with its logo on it arrived after the murders.*

His eyes widened with understanding. The logo. WLMT. They had to be at the radio station. He floored the accelerator, and the car jumped forward. "God, don't let me be too late."

As if from nowhere, doubt descended on him. He couldn't be sure Adam had taken C.J. to the radio station. He wanted to believe he was doing the right thing. If only he knew for sure. Once more he prayed. "Am I going in the right direction?"

The police radio crackled. "Attention all patrol cars in the vicinity of WLMT radio station. We have a report of a man holding two women prisoner inside the building. The man, Adam Connor, is suspected of three murders in Oxford and is wanted by the FBI. Approach with caution. He is armed and dangerous."

Mitch picked up his cell phone and hit speed dial for dispatch. "Oxford Police."

"Chet," Mitch yelled. "I'm on my way to the radio station. Who are the women he's holding?"

Chet hesitated for a moment. "C. J. Tanner and Gwen Anderson."

"How did you find out?"

"C.J. got away long enough to get to a phone and dial 9-1-1. She said Gwen's locked in a closet in her office."

Mitch swallowed back the fear rising in his throat. "Do you know the status of C.J. now?"

"No. The dispatcher told her to stay on the phone, but she said he was about to find her and she had to draw him away from Gwen. There's been no contact with her in the last few minutes. Officers are on the way, Mitch."

"I am, too." He started to hang up, but a thought crossed his mind. "Chet, call Dean Harwell and Bill Diamond. Tell them to meet us there."

"Ten-four."

His stomach roiled as he remembered how angry he'd been with C.J. earlier. The harsh words played in his mind, and regret consumed him. He couldn't live with himself if those were the last words he'd ever say to her. He had to stop Adam before he killed C.J. If Mitch could get there in time, he would spend the rest of his life trying to gain her forgiveness.

Mitch flipped the cell phone closed and looked up to the heavens again. With the department understaffed and the police cruisers scattered across the city, there was no telling how long it would take the first patrol car to get to the radio station.

Please watch over C.J., God.

TWENTY

The gun barrel in her back nudged C.J. toward the stairs. One thought replayed in her mind—stall. Give the police time to get here. She searched desperately for something to distract Adam. Her foot throbbed as she hobbled forward. She took one step, groaned and stopped.

"What's the matter?" Adam demanded.

She winced. "My foot. I must have hurt it when I fell."

Pressure on her back urged her forward. Adam grabbed her arm and twisted it behind her. "Quit wasting time. It's not going to matter in a few minutes whether it hurts or not."

C.J. grasped the railing of the stairs and pulled herself upward. At the second-floor landing, she stopped in the hallway. "My foot hurts. I can't go any farther."

His fingers wrenched her arm up her back. "Oh, yes, you can. We're going to the roof. The stairs are at the other end of the hall from the broadcast booths."

She shook her head. "We can't get up there. The door at the top of the stairs onto the roof is locked."

He laughed and leaned forward, his mouth at her ear. "But I have Harley's keys, and one of them is to the roof. Remember?"

C.J.'s heart plummeted to the bottom of her stomach. Adam had his scheme planned to the last detail, except for one thing—what she'd told Gwen. God was watching over them.

He pushed her forward, and she stumbled toward the end of the hallway. When they reached the door leading to the rooftop staircase, C.J. hesitated. Adam reached around her and turned the knob, then pushed the door open. The gun nudged her again. "Get moving."

She eased into the closetlike room that housed the steps and stared upward. The steps ended at a landing that opened onto the roof. Harley had taken her up there one day last summer when the roofers were patching some holes left by storms. She'd stood at the brick railing that circled the area and gazed over the rooftops of Oxford below. At the time it seemed like a beautiful sight. Now the prospect of walking on the roof conjured up an entirely different feeling.

"I said move!" Adam screamed in her ear.

With her head held high, she climbed upward. At the entrance to the roof she stopped as Adam reached around her. A sick feeling filled her stomach at the sight of Harley's keys in Adam's hand. She'd watched Harley jingle those keys many times.

The key slid into the lock, and the bolt clicked. Adam pushed the door open and shoved her through it. The door behind her closed, isolating Adam and her from the rest of the world. "Walk to the sign," Adam's voice growled.

She glanced at the large letters rising from the flat roof. When they had driven up to the station, three of the letters were lit. Now only two—the *L* and the *M*—burned against the night sky. The *W* blinked on and off like those on top of tall towers to warn planes. Its reflected light sparkled in the puddles dotting the roof. Patches of snow could still be seen in the crevices of the brick wall surrounding the roof, but the sun's rays had reduced most of the accumulation to small pockets of standing water all across the surface.

She took a step toward the sign and flinched. An icy coldness seeped through the bottom of her shoe, chilling her. Behind her, Adam stepped in the water and sent it rippling over the back of her shoe and onto her sock. She shivered and waded through the puddles toward the sign.

In the distance a siren wailed.

Adam didn't appear to notice the sound. He shoved her forward. "Turn around," he ordered.

Slowly, she faced him, her gaze sweeping over the gun he held in his hand.

There was nothing else she could do. She was about to die at the hands of the madman who'd killed before. She swallowed back the fear that rose in her throat.

She didn't want to die. Not this way. She wanted to share a lifetime with Mitch and grow old with him. How she wished he was here so she could tell him one more time how much she loved him.

Adam laughed and pointed the gun at her heart. "Prepare to die, C.J."

Mitch's car careened into the WLMT parking lot. No other police cars were anywhere in sight. He radioed in. "Officer twenty-seven at the radio station. Where's my backup?"

"On their way," a dispatcher answered. "ETA two minutes."

"Tell them to hurry. I'm going in alone."

Mitch jumped from the car, pulled his gun and ran to the front door. He crouched just below the glass panels and reached for the handle. Just as his hand touched it, he heard the roar of a car behind him. Dean Harwell's car screeched to a stop beside his. Dean, with gun drawn, was out of the car almost before it stopped.

"How'd you get here so fast?" Mitch asked.

"I live just two blocks away," Dean whispered. "Where's our guy now?"

Mitch shook his head. "I don't know. I'll lead the way to Gwen's office. Are you ready?"

Dean nodded, and the two of them, their guns clutched in front of them in a tactical position, slipped inside the building. On catlike feet they hurried to the staircase and started up, pausing from time to time to sweep the area with their weapons. No sound came from inside the building.

At the top of the stairs, Mitch motioned toward Gwen's office. A muffled click caught his attention. A door closing somewhere, he thought. They crept along the hall, paused outside the door and rushed in, their guns extended. Dean pulled a flashlight from his pocket and bounced the beam around the room. A quick survey revealed that no one was there. "C.J. said Gwen's in the closet. Cover me while I open the door."

He walked toward the closet, but stopped when something crunched under his foot. Dean aimed the light at the area, and Mitch glanced down. The broken remains of a lamp lay scattered about.

Mitch stepped over the shards to the closet. Keys dangled from the lock, and he turned the latch. A whimper escaped as he opened the door. Dean flashed the light into the small space, and Mitch's heart constricted at the sight of Gwen, her knees drawn up under her chin and her hands covering her eyes, cowering on the floor.

"No!" she wailed. "Get away from me!"

Mitch dropped down beside her and put his hand on her head. "Gwen, it's Mitch. You're all right now."

She looked up at him with terror-filled eyes. "Mitch, Adam has C.J. He's going to kill her and then kill me. He's going to leave a suicide note that says I'm Fala."

He leaned closer to her. "Where has he taken her?"

She began to cry. "T-to th-the r-r-roof. H-he s-said h-he was going to kill her by the s-sign."

Mitch jumped to his feet. "Dean, take care of Gwen. I have to find C.J."

"Don't you need me?" Dean called after him.

"Just take care of Gwen. The backup should be here any minute."

Mitch ran into the hall and stopped. At the end of the hallway he spied the door to the stairs ajar. He turned toward the landing, checked his gun and flattened his back against the wall. Slowly and deliberately he inched his way up toward the door that led to the rooftop.

C.J. held out her hand toward Adam. "Don't do this. You already have three murders to answer for. Don't make it another one."

Adam shook his head and chuckled. "Three? If you only knew how many there were before I came to Oxford."

"So you've done this before?"

"Many times. But I think this may be Fala's final game."

The sirens grew closer. "Adam, the police are on their way. You can't escape. Don't add more murders to your charges."

He turned his head and smiled. "Ah, the police. Well, they're going to be a little too late. By the time they make it up here, you'll be dead, and I'll be gone."

C.J. glanced at the side of the roof. "How? Are you going to fly?"

Adam wrinkled his brow as if in deep thought. "Um, maybe." Then he laughed. "No, C.J. I won't fly. But I always have a backup plan."

"What's that?"

He jingled Harley's keys in his hand. "I grew up in Montana, and I've been a rock climber ever since I can remember. I'm like a spider on sheer cliffs. I don't think the side of this building will give me any trouble. Harley's truck is not too far away. I'll be long gone before the police get here." He frowned. "Too bad, though. That means I'll have to leave Gwen in the closet."

The sirens wailed from the parking lot in front of the building. C.J. moved away from the sign. "Adam, no."

He leveled the gun at her. "Goodbye, C.J."

The door to the roof flew open. "Drop the gun, Adam!" Mitch yelled.

Adam's eyes grew wide. In one swift movement he grabbed C.J.'s arm and pulled her in front of him, the gun pressed to her head.

"Drop your gun if you want C.J. to live," Adam snarled.

Her heart pounding, C.J. stared at Mitch. His gaze flitted over her and settled on Adam. "Drop the weapon now, Adam. It'll go a lot better for you if you do."

Adam's arm tightened across her upper body, pinning both arms to her sides. Terror sucked the breath from her as the tip of the gun's barrel pressed against her temple. "You're in a no-win situation here, Mitch," Adam said. "You may be able to shoot me, but I'll take C.J. with me when I go. You don't want that, do you?"

C.J. squirmed in an effort to free herself, but Adam's arm crushed her. "Don't listen to him," she cried.

Mitch licked his lips and advanced a few steps. "Officers are entering the building now. You have nowhere to go. Give yourself up before it's too late."

Adam laughed and rubbed the barrel of the gun up and down the side of C.J.'s face. "Too late for what?" He stared at Mitch for a moment. "I'll tell you what, Mitch. You drop your gun, and I'll let C.J. go."

Fear struck C.J. "Don't believe him!"

Adam's maniacal laugh filled the air. "What choice does he have?"

Mitch looked at C.J. "Tell me what you'll do if I drop my gun."

"I'll release C.J., and I'll take your gun. Then I'll disappear over the side of this building and leave the two of you to live happily ever after. How about it, Mitch?"

"No," C.J. screamed. "Don't give up your gun! You can't trust him!"

Adam cocked the hammer of the gun. She struggled to pull away, but his strong arms held her upright. "I'm losing patience, Mitch," he yelled. "Throw the gun to me now, or C.J. dies."

Mitch raised his left hand and bent forward. With his right hand he laid the gun on the rooftop and slid it toward Adam, then stood. "Okay, there's my gun. Now let C.J. go, and you can get out of here before the other officers arrive."

"Tsk, tsk," Adam clucked. "You're way too trusting, old friend. My game's not through yet."

C.J.'s body jerked at the roar in her ears as the gun discharged. The bullet's impact propelled Mitch backward before he crumpled to the floor. For a moment she stared at his still body in disbelief. Mitch couldn't die without knowing how much she loved him. Tears welled in her eyes as she searched for any movement. There was none. If Mitch were dead, she didn't want to live, either.

"No!" she screamed, wrenching in Adam's grip. "You've killed him!"

"Shut up!" Adam yelled. "He was a fool to believe me. Now it's your turn."

His grip loosened, and she whirled around to face him, her right hand free. She twisted in an effort to escape, but he pulled her against him with the other arm. Something in her pocket gouged at her leg, and she gasped. A hot energy like molten lava flowed through her body, and she struggled in Adam's grip.

"Be still," he yelled, his hand slipping.

That split second was all she needed to plunge her free hand into her pocket and draw out the small canister of Mace attached to her key ring. Before Adam could regain his hold on her, her hand shot upward, she rammed the canister into his face, and she squirted the liquid right into his eyes.

"Aaargh!" Adam screamed and staggered backward. He clutched at his eyes. The gun he held fell from his hand, and C.J. scooped it up.

His balled fists dug into his tear-filled eyes. "You'll pay for this!"

C.J.'s shaking hand pointed the gun at him. "Stand still, Adam, or I'll shoot."

With a roar he pulled a knife from his pocket and began to swing it wildly in front of him. The blade swished through the air. "You haven't won the game yet," he said and took a step forward.

"Stay back!"

Blinded by the spray, he stopped and listened. "I know where you are. You can't escape me."

She moved to the side, her steps taking her closer to the sign. "Don't come any closer."

"You won't shoot," he screamed and leaped forward.

The pistol jerked in her hand as she pulled the trigger. A cry of pain ripped from Adam's throat, and he stumbled. Blood streamed down the side of his face where the bullet had grazed his head.

He whirled in a rage, slashing at empty air with his knife, tears still rolling from his eyes. C.J. raised the gun again and took a step backward. "Get back, or I'll shoot again!"

Adam lurched sideways, his shoes splashing the puddle of water around the sign. "I'll kill you, C.J."

Swinging the knife like a machete in front of him, he reeled forward. Suddenly, he lost his balance and stumbled toward the sign. He fought to regain his balance, but his body continued its fall. In a desperate effort, he reached out to grab hold of something to steady himself, but there was nothing to stop his descent. Nothing except the blinking letters of the sign. He plunged into them with a violent crash.

A popping sound filled the air, and sparks of electricity shot straight up. Adam's body gyrated as the voltage from the sign surged through him. A burning smell filled the air, and then his lifeless body dropped to the rooftop.

C.J's chest heaved in horror, and she shrank from the sight. She stared down at the pepper spray. Even though she'd been terrified, she'd used it. She'd reacted automatically when she saw Mitch...

Mitch! She whirled around in fear. He lay where he had fallen. "No," she whimpered and took a step toward him. "Please, God, don't let him be dead," she begged.

His leg twitched, and she ran forward. She dropped on her knees beside him and turned him over.

Blood poured from his side, and she pressed her hands against the wound. "God, take care of him. Give me a chance to tell him I love him."

The door to the roof flew open, and two officers rushed over to her. "What happened?"

"Mitch has been shot. He needs help."

The policeman turned his mouth to his lapel mic. "Officer down on the WLMT roof. We need an ambulance right away."

Mitch stirred and opened his eyes. He blinked and stared at her for a moment. "What happened?"

The tears she'd been holding back poured from her eyes. "Adam shot you, but it's all right now. Help is on the way."

He tried to push himself into a sitting position, but one of the officers helped her restrain him. "Don't move. Wait for the paramedics."

As she grabbed his hand and began to kiss it, he winced and frowned. "Are you all right?"

She wiped at the tears on her cheeks. "I'm fine. When Adam shot you, I thought you were dead, and I wanted to die, too."

"Why?" he whispered.

"Because I didn't want you to die and not know how much I love you." She began to cry again.

His eyes filled with wonder. "I never thought I'd hear you say those words again. Do you really mean it?"

Before she could answer, the door to the roof opened again, and two men dressed in dark suits entered. Mitch stared upward as one of the men stopped and knelt beside him. "Bill," he said. "We got Fala." He glanced back at C.J. and smiled. "Or maybe I should say C.J. did."

The man stuck out his hand. "Bill Diamond, Miss Tanner. The officers downstairs told me what happened. Good work."

She smiled and reached for his hand. "Thank you. I'm just glad we lived through the ordeal."

Bill turned his head to stare at the body by the sign. "Jack Horn finally got what he deserved. There'll be a lot of families across the country glad to hear the news." He stood and walked toward the sign to join the officers there.

C.J. turned her attention back to Mitch and held his hand until the paramedics arrived. She stood aside as they worked with him, checking his vital signs and inserting an IV. When they picked up the stretcher and started down the stairs, she glanced back at the officers and the two FBI agents who stood around Adam's body.

The WLMT sign blazed its brilliant light across the night sky—all four of the letters lit now. She recalled Harley telling her he suspected a short was causing the problem with the sign. At the time she had been upset that he hadn't had it fixed, but now she realized a higher plan had ruled the decision for the repair work to be delayed.

C.J. smiled and looked up at the sky. Mary, Caleb and Harley had died for no reason, but their murders had not gone unpunished. She shuddered once more and followed the stretcher down the stairs.

C.J. stepped into the hallway of the second floor behind the paramedics, but stopped at the sight of Gwen, a blanket wrapped around her shoulders, leaning against the wall. A man with long hair and a beard stood beside her, holding a cup of water. They looked up as the stretcher came into sight. Gwen gave a cry and ran toward her. They wrapped their arms around each other and cried for several moments before C.J. pulled away. "I have to go. They're taking Mitch to the hospital."

The man who'd been standing by Gwen nodded. "I'm Dean Harwell, Miss Tanner. They won't let you ride in the ambulance. I'd be glad to take you and Gwen."

C.J. heard the front door downstairs opening. "Then let's go. I want to see Mitch again before they put him in the ambulance."

She ran down the stairs, Dean and Gwen right behind her. At the door she stopped in amazement at the crowd gathered outside. Policemen formed two lines across the front of the building to hold the people back.

"What in the world?" she said.

Dean chuckled. "Reporters. They showed up to see how C. J. Tanner caught the mysterious Fala."

C.J. stared in disbelief for a moment and then pushed the door open. Pandemonium broke out as she rushed toward the stretcher.

"C.J.!" The cry erupted from the crowd. "C.J., give us a statement."

She shook her head and ran toward Mitch. The paramedics stopped at the back of the ambulance and reached up to open the doors.

"C.J.! C.J.! What was it like to come face-to-face with Fala?"

Mitch smiled up at her. "Go on and talk to them. I'll see you at the hospital."

She leaned over and kissed him on the cheek, then turned to the crowd. "I want my listeners to know that I've learned a lot through this experience. I started my program to talk about how the citizens of Oxford could work together to make our city a better place to live. We may not be perfect, but if we pull together, we can defeat the Falas who would put the lives of our loved ones at risk. I hope this has brought us all closer together so that we can make this a safe place for our families." C.J. glanced over her shoulder. "I have to go to the hospital now."

The paramedics slammed the ambulance door, and C.J. ran with Dean and Gwen toward Dean's car. She stopped before climbing into the backseat and stared up at the sky. When they'd left Adam's house, she'd thought tonight might be the last time she would ever see the stars twinkling. Now they would always remind her of how much God loved her.

She could hardly wait to tell Mitch what she had discovered tonight.

C.J. adjusted the blinds in the hospital room to keep the sun's rays out of Mitch's eyes. She checked the thermostat and lifted the top of the water pitcher to make sure it still contained ice.

Picking up a pillow, she wedged it under Mitch's head. "Are you comfortable?" she asked. "Tell me what you need, and I'll get it." She grasped the blanket and drew it up over him.

Mitch chuckled. "I'm fine, C.J. You've been like a mother hen all morning. Quit hovering over me. You've been here all night. Why don't you go home and get some rest?"

She pulled a chair beside his bed, dropped onto it and rubbed her eyes. "I am tired, but I couldn't leave until I knew you were going to be all right."

He directed the smile that she loved so much at her. "I can't tell you how much it meant to me to find you waiting when I came back from surgery last night."

C.J. remembered the hours she'd spent waiting with Dean and Gwen for the doctor to tell her Mitch's wound was not life threatening. When they'd brought him from recovery, though, he'd looked pale and vulnerable, and she'd known she couldn't leave him.

"I wanted to be here," she said.

He smiled again, and her heart almost burst with the love she felt for him. He reached for her hand and laced her fingers with his. "Every time I woke up last night, you were sitting in that chair. It made me very happy."

"I'm glad."

They sat in silence for a moment, and C.J. wondered what he was thinking. When they'd been on the roof, she'd told him she loved him. He hadn't said those words to her, and she wondered if he ever would. Maybe she'd waited too long, pushed him away too many times. She had to prepare herself for the possibility that Mitch's love for her had died.

The thought pierced her heart. Then she remembered the peace she'd discovered the night before. If Mitch didn't love her, she would be all right because she wasn't alone anymore. Now the spirit of God lived in her, and with His help she could face anything.

She took a deep breath. It was time to tell Mitch everything.

C.J. gripped his hand tighter and leaned toward him. "When you were lying on the roof last night, do you remember what I said to you?"

He nodded. "You said you loved me."

"Yes. I want you to know that I've never stopped loving you, not even when I broke our engagement."

A frown wrinkled his forehead. "Then why did you do it?"

"For many reasons. At the time I told myself it was because I thought you were being unfair with your objections to my radio program. I was determined no man was ever going to treat me the way my father treated my mother."

"You've never talked to me about your childhood. Not even when I asked you."

C.J. swallowed the tears she felt rising, and bit her lip. "I know, but I want to tell you now."

For the next few minutes she told him of the beautiful woman and handsome man who had been her parents, and how wonderful life had been until they became obsessed with getting the next drug fix. She related her mother's beatings, the nights she stayed alone in strange rooms waiting for them to return and other nights when she cowered under the covers trying to block out the noise of the partying in the next room. She ended with her mother abandoning her in a mall.

With tears streaming down her face, she leaned forward. "I've lived with those memories for years. I couldn't understand what kind of God would let a mother desert her child."

His face was a mask of sorrow. "Oh, C.J., what you must have suffered."

She reached for a tissue on the bedside table and wiped her eyes. "When God didn't answer my prayers, I closed the door to Him. Last night, though, I found out He'd never left me. When I needed Him, He was with me and brought me through the worst time of my life."

Mitch grimaced in pain as he tried to push himself up in bed. "Are you telling me that you're a believer?"

C.J. nodded, and gently restrained him. "Yes. I asked God to forgive me for doubting Him, and He gave me another chance."

Relief lined his face as he sank back on the pillow. "I've prayed for this, but I was beginning to think it would never happen," he said.

She got up from the chair and walked to the window. She stared out for a few moments before she turned back to Mitch. "I had a lot of time to talk to God last night while I was sitting beside you. I poured out all the hurt that I've stored up for years, and I listened to what He'd been trying to tell me."

"What was that?"

"My parents' choices hurt God as much as they did me. He loved them even when they were destroying themselves, and He tried to reach them, but they wouldn't listen. When I thought He'd forgotten me, He was right there with me. He was the one who got me though the years in the foster homes, gave me the will to excel in school and the ability to work my way through college. He also gave me you, and my job at the radio station. And I didn't really appreciate any of it because I was filled with self-pity because He didn't perform a miracle in my parents' lives."

Mitch held out his hand. "I'm so sorry I didn't help you more."

C.J. walked back to the bed and grasped his hand. "But you did. You're not like my father, Mitch. God sent you to me so I could see what a really good man is like. You kept giving me the message that God still loved me, but I wouldn't listen." She took a deep breath. "Mitch, I'm sorry I ever doubted you, too. I love you so much. God gave me another chance. Will you forgive me?"

His eyes lit up, and he placed her hand on his chest. "Can you feel my heart pounding? That's because I'm so happy. Of course I forgive you." He brought her hand to his mouth and kissed his fingers. "But C.J., you aren't the only one who made mistakes in our relationship."

"What do you mean?" she murmured.

Mitch sighed. "I was pigheaded about you doing the radio program and didn't understand how important it was to you. The night I sat beside you at the broadcast I saw how good you are at what you do, and I was ashamed of the way I'd acted. God gave you a special gift, and I tried to make you give it up because I was afraid for you. I should have known that if God meant for you to do it, He would take care of you. So, can you forgive me?"

She scooted closer to him. "So does that mean you love me, too?"

He reached up with one arm and pulled her face close to his. "I've never quit loving you. Don't you ever leave me again."

"I won't," she whispered.

He pulled her closer. "So I'll ask you for the second time. Will you marry me?"

She placed her palms on either side of his face and stared down at him. "Yes, yes, yes."

Behind them the door opened, and a nurse stepped into the room. She chuckled, and pointed to a small paper cup she held. "I have your medicine, but it looks like you're busy. I'll come back in a few minutes."

C.J. turned back to Mitch, and he pulled her to him. "What you've given me today is better than any medicine a doctor could order."

Their lips met, and for the first time in months C.J. felt at peace. When Mitch released her, she smiled. "I was just thinking, God brought us through a terrible time. He must have something wonderful planned for our lives."

Mitch smiled. "I can hardly wait to see what it is."

* * * * *

Dear Reader,

Thank you for taking time to read *Final Warning*. I hope you
enjoyed it and found something you could relate to in your life.

As I wrote this story, the characters became special to me,
and I agonized at times over their problems. Bringing two
complex people together isn't easy, even in fiction. Like Mitch
and C.J., we, too, are products of our previous experiences.

In John 13:34, Jesus said, "A new commandment I give
unto you, That ye love one another; as I have loved you."
These words provide the answer to how we form relation-
ships, how we learn to love and be loved. Only when we love
as Jesus loved us can we know true fulfillment in our lives.

C.J. and Mitch learned this. I hope you have in your life,
too. It is my prayer that you may experience the true peace
that God's love can bring.

Sandra Robbins

QUESTIONS FOR DISCUSSION

1. At the beginning of *Final Warning,* C.J. is dealing with the heartache over her broken engagement. Have you ever faced a personal problem that caused anguish in your life? How did you deal with it?

2. Mitch thought it was important for both parties in a relationship to be believers. What do you think? What does the Bible say about this?

3. How did C.J.'s childhood experiences affect her ability to trust in a future with Mitch? How can a person overcome hurtful memories?

4. C.J. thought Myra was interested in Mitch romantically, and became jealous of her. Have you ever been jealous of another person? What are some of the bitter fruits that jealousy produces in our lives?

5. Do you think Mitch's concerns about C.J.'s radio show are reasonable? Why or why not?

6. Have you, like C.J., ever experienced a friend's death from an act of violence? How did it affect you?

7. Drugs have become readily available in American society. What can we do as Christians to combat this growing problem? How do we stop dealers like Jimmy Carpenter who are intent on selling our children drugs?

8. C.J. and Gwen found out what it was like to lose their jobs because of someone's deceit. Have you ever been treated unfairly in the workplace? How did you address the problem?

9. Although C.J. turned away from God when she was a child, she found that He had never abandoned her. Do you rely on your own strength and wisdom at times, or do you trust all your needs to Him?

10. When C.J. thought she was going to die, she felt the presence of God. Have you ever faced a life-threatening situation? What emotions did that situation make you feel?

11. II Timothy 2:13 says, "If we believe not, yet ye abideth faithful: he cannot deny himself." What does this verse mean to you?

*A thrilling romance between a British nurse and
an American cowboy on the African plains.*

Turn the page for a sneak preview of
THE MAVERICK'S BRIDE
by Catherine Palmer.
*Available September 2009
from Love Inspired® Historical.*

Adam hoisted himself onto the balcony, swinging one leg at a time over the rail. He hoped he hadn't been spotted by a compound guard.

But the sight of Emma Pickering peering out from behind the curtain put his concerns to rest. He had done the right thing.

"Good morning, Miss Pickering." He leaned against the white window frame.

"Mr. King." She was almost breathless. "I cannot speak with you."

"But I need to talk. Mind if I come inside?"

"Indeed, sir, you may not take another step! Are you mad?"

He couldn't hold back a grin. "No more than most. I figure anyone who would leave home and travel all the way to Africa has to be a little off-kilter."

"You refer to me, I suppose? I'll have you know I'm here for a very good reason."

"Railway inspection, is it? Or nursing?"

Emma looked even better than he had thought she might—and he had thought about her a lot.

"Speaking of nursing," he ventured.

"Mr. King, I have already told you I'm unavailable. Now please let yourself down by that…that rope thing, and—"

"My lasso?"

"You must go down again, sir. This is unseemly."

Emma was edgy this morning. Almost frightened. Different from the bold young woman he had met yesterday.

He couldn't let that concern him. Last night after he left the consulate, he had made up his mind to keep things strictly business with Emma Pickering.

"I'll leave after I've had my say," he told her. "This is important."

"Speak quickly, sir. My father must not find you here."

"With all due respect, Emma, do you think I'm concerned about what your father thinks?"

"You may not care, but I do. What do you want from me?"

"I need a nurse."

"A nurse? Are you ill?"

"Not for me. I have a friend—at my ranch."

Her eyes deepened in concern as she let the curtain drop a little. "What sort of illness does your friend have? Can you describe it?"

Adam looked away. How could he explain the situation without scaring her off?

"It's not an illness. It's more like…"

Searching for the right words, he turned back to Emma. But at the first full sight of her face, he reached through the open window and pulled the curtain out of her hands.

"Emma, what happened to you?" He caught her arm and drew her toward him. "Who did this?"

She raised her hand in a vain effort to cover her cheek and eye. "It's nothing," she protested, trying to back away. "Please, Mr. King, you must not…"

Even as she tried to speak, he stepped through the balcony door and gathered her into his arms. Brushing back the hair from her cheek, he noted the swelling and the darkening stain around it.

"Emma," he growled. "Who did this to you?"

She fell motionless, silent in his embrace. No wonder she had shied like a scared colt. She hadn't wanted him to know.

Torn with dismay that anyone would ever harm this beautiful woman, he felt an irresistible urge to kiss her.

"Emma, you have to tell me...." Realization flooded through him. A pompous, nattily dressed English railroad tycoon had struck his own daughter.

"Leave me, I beg you. You have no place here."

"Emma, wait. Listen to me." Adam caught her wrists and pulled her back toward him. He'd never been a man to think things through too carefully. He did what felt right.

"I want you to come with me," he told her. "I need your help. Let's go right now. Emma, I'll take care of you."

"I don't need anyone to take care of me," she shot back. "God is watching over me."

"Emma!" Both turned toward the open door where Emma's sister stood, eyes wide.

"Emma, go with him!" Cissy crossed the room toward them. "Run away with him, Emma. It's your chance to escape—to become a nurse, as you've always wanted. You'll be safe at last, and you can have your dream."

Emma turned back to Adam.

"Come on," he urged her. "Let's get moving."

* * * * *

*Will Emma run away with Adam and finally realize
her dreams of becoming a nurse?
Find out in THE MAVERICK'S BRIDE,
available in September 2009
only from Love Inspired® Historical.*

Love Inspired®

HEARTWARMING INSPIRATIONAL ROMANCE

Get more of the heartwarming
inspirational romance stories that
you love and cherish, beginning
in July with SIX NEW titles,
available every month from
the Love Inspired® line.

Also look for our other
Love Inspired® genres, including:

Love Inspired® Suspense:
Enjoy four contemporary tales of intrigue
and romance every month.

Love Inspired® Historical:
Travel to a different time with two powerful
and engaging stories of romance, adventure
and faith every month.

*Available every month wherever books are sold,
including most bookstores, supermarkets,
drugstores and discount stores.*

www.SteepleHill.com

Steeple
Hill

LIINCREASE2